Pepper had a wonderful rocking canter, but nobody would know that looking at Skye Ransom. He rode Pepper as if he were Ichabod Crane being chased by the headless horseman. There was a look of pure terror on his face.

"Cut!" Oliver cried out. "Something wrong, Skye?"

"No," Skye said, but it was clear that there was.

"Is the horse going too fast for you?" Oliver asked.

"No," Skye said. Lisa could tell that Skye was very uncomfortable about something, but she also knew that he was too much of a professional to let his problems cause trouble on the set. "Let's try it again, Oliver," he suggested.

Oliver agreed and the scene was set up again. Lisa returned to the stable, prepared to step out on cue. From the shadows, she watched Skye's approach. The second time wasn't any better than the first. The problem was that Skye was scared, pure and simple.

If only The Saddle Club could think of a way to help . . .

THE SADDLE CLUB

STAR RIDER

BONNIE BRYANT

A SKYLARK BOOK
NEW YORK • TORONTO • LONDON • SYDNEY • AUCKLAND

I would like to express my special thanks to Ellen Krieger for her contribution to this story. Cheers!

—B.B.H.

RL 5, 009–012

STAR RIDER

A Skylark Book / December 1991

LISA ATWOOD PATTED the black colt reassuringly.

"Don't worry, Samson," she told him. "Everything's going to be fine."

He swished his tail. His ears flicked.

"That means he's listening," Carole Hanson told her friend.

Lisa could tell. The young horse had watched every move she'd made since she'd entered his paddock. He never even looked at his mother, a palomino camed Delilah, who was observing the training session intently from the other side of a fence.

Lisa moved around to face Samson, holding a bridle and a bit in her hands. She wanted him to be able to see and smell the tack so he wouldn't be frightened when she put it on him. He glanced at the bit and bridle and took two steps back. She patted him again.

Although Lisa's two best friends, Carole and Stevie Lake, were just a few feet away, Lisa was concentrating so hard on Samson that it was as if they were the only two beings in the world.

"It's just me," she said, speaking in a low voice, calmly stepping toward the retreating colt. He responded by stopping. "I'm going to teach you something, and you're going to show me what a good pupil you are."

The words flowed automatically. Lisa knew that *what* she was saying to Samson really didn't matter. What was important was that he heard her voice and sensed the calm in it. If he heard uncertainty or fear, he'd flee.

As Samson stood still, Lisa stood on his left side. She held the bit of the bridle in her left hand and the crownpiece in her right. Without hesitation she put the bit by his mouth, poising the crownpiece to go over his ears when the bit was in place. Samson was surprised and opened his mouth to protest. Before he knew what had happened, she slipped the bit into his mouth and then very quickly slid the crownpiece into place over his ears. He was in a bridle and all that was left to do was to convince him he wanted to stay that way until she could get the thing buckled.

"It's what all the well-dressed horses are wearing this

STAR RIDER

year," she said to Samson, imitating a fashion show emcee. "The modest mini, with a slight metallic accent—perfect for the afternoon outing or a morning in the field. No wardrobe would be complete without it."

Lisa quickly buckled the bridle and then took the reins. Samson chomped curiously at the unfamiliar piece of metal in his mouth, but he stood willingly.

"Ta-dah!" Stevie called out from the fence where she and Carole sat.

"Nice job!" Carole chimed in. "You're a natural-born trainer."

"Oh, it wasn't that big of a deal," Lisa said, leading Samson over to the fence. "After all, he's been wearing a halter for months now."

"There's a big difference between a halter and a bit, and Samson is smart enough to know it. You did a perfect job of introducing him to his new tack," Carole said.

Lisa was almost embarrassed by Carole's compliment. The three girls were best friends and they were all good horseback riders. They loved horses so much that they'd created The Saddle Club, which had only two rules: Members had to be horse crazy, and they had to be willing to help one another out. Lisa was the newest rider of the three, but she worked hard at it and had learned a lot in the short time she'd been riding. Lisa was a straight-A student in school and approached everything she did logically and analytically. It didn't surprise those around her that she usually succeeded at things she tried. It always seemed to surprise Lisa, though.

Stevie, on the other hand, was a schemer. When there was a problem to be solved, Stevie could always think of a way to solve it, and it usually involved getting everybody into hot water. Carole and Lisa didn't mind that too much. Being anywhere with Stevie was fun—even hot water.

Carole was the most serious rider of the three. She'd been raised on Marine Corps bases, where her widowed father was a colonel, and had learned to ride the military horses as a very little girl. When she grew up, Carole was going to be a trainer, or a vet, or a championship rider, or a breeder—or all of them!

"Can I try leading him now?" Stevie asked. Lisa nodded and handed her the reins.

Samson seemed so preoccupied with the strange feel of the bit in his mouth that he just followed willingly. Lisa climbed up onto the paddock fence and sat next to Carole.

"He's going to be a breeze to train with a saddle when the time comes," she observed.

"Only if he's got good trainers," Carole said.

"He will, because he'll have us," Lisa reminded her.

"And we're the best," Stevie added, returning with Samson to where her friends sat on the fence.

"Speaking of being the best, didn't you guys promise to help me plan Dad's surprise birthday party?" Carole asked.

"We did help you," Stevie said. "We reminded you to send out the invitations, didn't we?"

"Big help," Carole said. "Tell you what, I'll walk Samson in a circle now while you two figure out exactly what we're going to do to make Dad's fortieth birthday the best ever."

Carole slid off the fence, landing on the soft earth of the paddock. Samson watched while Stevie handed the reins to Carole. He seemed vaguely aware of the fact that the reins were attached to the odd thing in his mouth. He chomped at it unsuccessfully.

"Forty!" Stevie said, climbing up next to Lisa. "It sounds awfully old."

"My dad turned forty two years ago," Lisa said. "He talked about it for months."

"What did you do for a party?" Stevie asked.

"Nothing," Lisa said. Then a thought occurred to her. "Maybe that's why he talked about it so much! But he said he didn't want us to do anything."

"They always say that," Stevie said.

"And they never mean it," Lisa added.

"Well, Colonel Hanson is a terrific guy, and I want to help Carole make this his best birthday ever."

"Me, too," Lisa agreed.

Colonel Hanson was a favorite with all the riders at Pine Hollow Stable, where The Saddle Club rode and where he was one of the parent volunteers for the pony club, Horse Wise. He was a special favorite of Stevie's because they shared a passion for 1950s trivia and old jokes. Sometimes Carole had trouble shaking her father from the phone when Stevie called. Stevie and Colonel Hanson seemed to have an unlimited supply of grape and elephant jokes to try on one another.

"You know," Stevie began, "if we're going to help Carole throw the party, we're talking about decorating and cooking—"

"And cleaning up," Lisa said sensibly.

"The trouble is, the only thing I know how to cook is Rice Krispies treats," Stevie said.

"Well, then it's a good thing Colonel Hanson really loves them," Lisa told her.

"Lisa! Phone call!" Lisa looked to see Mrs. Reg. She was the mother of Max Regnery, the man who owned Pine Hollow. Mrs. Reg served as the stable manager. She didn't like to think of herself as a telephone operator and usually refused to hunt down somebody to take a phone call. Lisa was concerned.

"Is it an emergency?" she called, running toward Mrs. Reg.

"Nope, but it's long distance—from California. You'd better hurry."

Lisa did. She ran so fast, she was totally breathless by the time she reached Mrs. Reg's desk.

"Hello?" she almost gasped into the phone.

"Is this Lisa Atwood?" a voice asked. It was a gentle and familiar voice, but Lisa couldn't quite place it.

"Yes, who's this?" she asked.

"It's Skye—Skye Ransom," the voice informed her. "Remember me?"

"Really?" Lisa couldn't believe it. Of course she remembered him. Skye Ransom was a famous teen movie actor whom she and her friends had gotten to know when they were on a trip to New York City to attend the horse show there. The girls had met him when he'd been trying to learn to ride horseback because he was starring in a movie that required him to ride. Skye hadn't wanted to admit to anyone that he didn't know a thing about horses. The Saddle Club had taught him everything he'd needed to know. They hadn't really expected to hear from him again, although Lisa *had* written him a letter to say that she'd seen the movie eight times when it came out.

"You don't recognize my voice after seeing my movie eight times?" Skye teased.

Lisa laughed. "I recognize it. I just don't believe it! What are you calling for and how did you find me here?"

"I tracked you down," he said. "See, I'm doing another horse movie."

"You want more riding tips?" Lisa asked.

"Well, partly that," he said. "I do need more riding tips."

"Look, my friends and I would love to give you lessons, but wouldn't it make more sense to find an instructor in California?"

"I could do that, I suppose," he said. "But if I did, I'd have to take lessons long distance. See . . ."

"STEVIE! CAROLE! GET this!" Lisa shrieked as she dashed back to Samson's paddock. "You're never going to believe it! Never!"

"What?" Carole asked.

"It's incredible!" Lisa said.

"What's incredible?" Stevie asked.

"You won't believe it!" Lisa repeated.

"If you won't tell us what it is, we won't have a chance to believe it," Stevie said sensibly.

Lisa brought herself to a halt, and gulped. She couldn't get the words out.

"Who was calling?" Carole asked. She thought maybe if she could just get Lisa started, she might learn what was going on.

"It was Skye," Lisa began.

"Ransom?" Carole and Stevie asked in a single voice. Lisa nodded.

"Yeah, Skye Ransom. He was calling *me*. From California. Where he is—"

"This could take all day," Stevie said.

Lisa ignored it. She concentrated on getting her news out. "—but he won't be in California for long. See, he's making another horse movie. It's a sequel to the one he was making in New York. Only this time it's going to be shot in . . . in . . . ."

"Virginia?" Carole asked.

Lisa nodded. "Yeah, somewhere in Virginia. Anyway, he wanted to know if I—and you two—could help him some more. Can you believe it? See? I told you you wouldn't believe it. Isn't it incredible?"

"Wow," Carole said.

"Outstanding!" Stevie added, but then her face fell.

"Virginia's a big state, you know. He could be miles from here."

"Wherever he is in Virginia, it's closer to us than California, isn't it?" Carole reasoned.

"Oh, yeah," Stevie said. "That's definitely true."

Carole felt a tug at her hand, then. She had almost forgotten that she was holding Samson's reins. Before she could do anything about it, Samson tugged them out of her hand and began darting around the paddock, dragging the reins. He nearly stepped on them several times.

"Oh, no!" Carole said. She realized right away that Samson was so unaccustomed to the leather straps that he might very well trip himself.

Nobody needed to say anything. The Saddle Club immediately knew what to do. Working quickly and wordlessly, the three of them cornered Samson in the paddock. Lisa began speaking to him in her soft, reassuring voice. His ears flicked curiously. She approached him slowly from his right side. She kept talking as she neared him. She held his attention so that he never noticed that Carole was actually much closer, on his left side. Just as he was about to dart away, Carole reached out and grasped his reins.

"Good boy," Lisa said. She patted him. He seemed a little disappointed that the excitement was over so fast.

The Saddle Club was relieved they had kept him from creating more excitement.

While Lisa patted Samson some more, Carole unbuckled the bridle and released the bit from his mouth. He shifted his jaw around cautiously and seemed satisfied that everything was normal. Carole patted his flank and Stevie opened the gate to let Samson back into the paddock with his mother.

"What a team!" Lisa remarked.

"We're really something!" Carole said. "We can train colts, we can even instruct famous movie stars!"

"And cater birthday parties," Stevie added.

"Let's face it, girls," Lisa said. "We're The Saddle Club. We can do anything."

"WHAT'S ALL THE noise out here?" Max Regnery demanded, storming from the stable to where the girls were still celebrating their own brilliance. "The horses are all nervous and edgy, and you three are giggling and shouting. I can't have—"

The girls glanced at one another. It was true that they'd been making some noise, but it didn't seem that the horses had been in the least bit upset until Max marched through the stable, swinging his arms and bellowing at them.

Max was a wonderful teacher and a good friend to all the riders. Most of the time he was pretty relaxed and understanding. The exception to that was when it came to horses. Riding and caring for horses always came first with Max. That included classes, too. He was a no-

nonsense instructor. When Max said no talking, he meant it. More than one chatty student had found herself ousted from Max's class until she was prepared to concentrate the way Max wanted her to. Now he had that same no-nonsense look on his face, but the girls hadn't been breaking any of his rules.

"I'm sorry, Max," Carole said. "We got a little carried away, but I didn't realize the horses were upset by what we were doing."

"Just what were you doing?" Max asked, calming down a little bit.

"We were putting a bit on Samson," Stevie said. "He was really good, too. And then, when we took it off, he almost seemed to miss the feel of it in his mouth."

"He was so cute, Max. You just wouldn't believe it," Lisa said, patting the colt through the fence.

Max looked at Samson and smiled. It was almost impossible to watch the gentle colt and not smile.

"You three are doing good work with him," Max said. "I'm sorry. I think maybe it was the fact that I'm upset that upset the horses."

"What are you upset about?" Carole asked.

"I have a decision to make," he said. Then he looked around at the interested faces of his three most eager riders. "Maybe you can help me."

"We'd be glad to try," Lisa said.

"Well, we can talk while we work," Max said. "The farrier will be here later today, and I want to make sure we check all the shoes before he gets here. Help me round up some of the horses in the north paddock, okay?"

That was just like Max. He could talk and ask the girls for advice, but he couldn't bear the idea that anybody might just stand and talk while there was work to do.

The girls agreed to his terms and followed him to the north paddock, where six horses were enjoying the freedom of the pasture.

The girls rounded up the horses and contained them near the entrance while Max checked their shoes. The farrier, or blacksmith, came to Pine Hollow about once a week, and Max wanted to be sure that all the horses who needed shoes or repair work were ready for him.

"I had a phone call from a man named Blake Dithers. He makes movies."

Three pairs of human ears perked up.

"It seems he's looking for a stable in Virginia where he can spend a week—Monday to Friday—making a movie that has to do with horses. Somehow, the name of this place came up. . . ."

The girls looked at one another. They all had the same thought.

"Anyway, the man seemed to think I should know

about this movie. He kept talking about the star—his name is Cloud or something like that."

"Skye," Lisa said.

"Oh," Max said, realizing that he knew the name, too. "I remember. He's the actor you girls met in New York, right?" They nodded. "Did you have anything to do with this?" They shook their heads. "Well, maybe it's just coincidence."

"It has to be," Stevie assured him. "None of us has heard from Skye since New York—until today, of course."

Max nodded absently. "Of course," he said. "But there's a problem. This guy, Dithers, seemed sure I'd want to go along with his movie plans."

"You *do*, don't you?" Lisa asked, horrified at the realization that there was a real risk Max would turn Mr. Dithers down.

"Do you know how much work it would be to have this place turned into a movie set?" Max asked. "It would be totally disruptive to our regular riders. The movie people would almost shut the place down while they had the run of it."

"They'll pay, won't they?" Stevie asked.

"That's not my main concern," Max said. "But, of course, they'll pay. When Dithers got the idea I wasn't totally enthusiastic, he practically doubled the amount of money he was offering. Yes, they'll pay. A lot."

"Think what you could do with the money!" said Stevie, the pragmatist.

"Think how much work it's going to be!" Max countered.

If ever there was a time for a Saddle Club meeting, this was it. The girls just had to have a chance to talk.

"Uh, Max, I think those three horses over there ought to be checked," Stevie said, pointing to two bays and a chestnut on the far side of the paddock. "We'll go get them for you, okay?"

Max nodded. The three girls headed for the horses—out of earshot of Max.

"Isn't this wonderful?" Lisa asked, trotting alongside her friends.

"We've just got to convince him," Stevie said.

"Well, we're The Saddle Club. We can do anything," Lisa reminded her friends.

"The only thing that's going to convince Max is if he's sure the movie company won't disrupt the running of Pine Hollow and that the horses will all be safe and well tended."

"How can we convince him of those things?" Lisa asked.

"By assuring him we can do it ourselves," Carole said.

"Ah, we have to be logical about this?" Stevie asked.

Carole nodded. Then both of them turned to Lisa.

"We're going to need a work schedule," she said. "We may even have to get some of the other riders to help."

"Do you think we can do that?" Carole asked.

Stevie gave her a withering look. "When it means they'll have a chance to actually see Cloud?—I mean Skye?"

The three girls giggled. They were sure Max could remember Skye's name just as well as they could. He was just being funny, and four could play at that game.

"Let's get the horses over to Max and make a proposal," Carole said. She whistled to get the horses' attention. They willingly came to her call and followed the girls back to the paddock gate, where Max was waiting for them.

"We want to make a deal," Carole begin. "Lisa will tell you about it."

Almost unconsciously, Lisa stood up straight and brushed off her blouse. She took a deep breath and began.

"We've decided that it would be a good idea for Pine Hollow to have Mr. Dithers's movie company here," she began.

Max looked at the three of them. "Oh, have you?" he said.

Lisa nodded. "It would be good publicity and it would

make extra money for you. That might make it possible for you to make some improvements—not that this place isn't already perfect—but there's a mare you've been wanting to buy, and the feed shed needs a new roof, you know, stuff like that. Anyway, we propose to offer the services of Pine Hollow's young riders, starting with this group, working in organized shifts, to help make things run smoothly for the duration."

Max seemed interested. "You girls are willing to do all this work just so I can put a new roof on the feed shed?" he asked.

"Definitely," Stevie chimed in. "The feed shed is important to all of us."

"And so is the mare you might buy," Carole added.

"Just for the experience of hard work," Lisa said. "We really care, you know?"

"I had no idea how devoted you were to Pine Hollow," Max said.

"Oh, we definitely are," Stevie assured him.

"It will be a lot of work," Max said.

"Like what?" Stevie asked.

"Like grooming, cleaning stalls, tacking and untacking for the riders in the movie. There will be a lot of grounds-keeping. The place will have to be spotless. There may be some painting that we have to do, and I'm sure there will be special training required of some of the horses, maybe even lessons for some of the performers."

"No problem," Lisa said. "We can get you a grounds crew, trainers, or grooms at the drop of a hat."

"And lessons for the performers?" Max asked. "Who is going to take care of that chore?"

Three hands went up at once.

"All right," Max said. "I'll call Dithers and tell him it's okay. He won't believe that my riders are so devoted they'll give up their own lessons just to pitch in for his movie."

"Oh, thank you, Max!" Lisa said, feeling relieved. "You won't be sorry!"

Max laughed. "I probably won't be, but you all may be. You're going to be working very hard just to have a chance to see your friend, Cloud."

"Skye," Lisa corrected him automatically. "You think that's the only reason we're willing to work?"

"Probably not the only one," Max said. "But to tell you the truth, I didn't believe the one about the roof on the feed shed."

"Weak, huh?" Lisa asked.

"It was a nice try," Max said. "Now, I'll make a confession. I had already decided to say yes to Dithers. It will be interesting to learn about movie-making, and I thought perhaps you three might be willing to work for free just to get another close-up look at this guy, Cloud."

"Skye!" Lisa said, exasperated. "And, yes, we would. After all, Skye is our friend. He's actually even a sort of pupil of ours. . . ."

"Ah, yes, and I recall tales of how much fun you three had riding around New York City in his stretch limo, don't I?" Max asked. Before the girls had a chance to protest, Max changed the subject. "Two of these horses need shoes, the others are fine. Bring Barq and Coconut into the stable for the farrier, okay?"

"Okay," Carole agreed, but before she said it, Max was gone, disappearing into his office to call Mr. Dithers.

"This is incredible," Lisa said.

"Yes," Stevie agreed. "And what's incredible about it is that I think we just got outfoxed by Max."

"Ah, but think how great it will be to have a new roof on the feed shed!" Carole teased.

The three of them laughed.

3

STEVIE, CAROLE, AND Lisa waited impatiently for the first signs of arrival of the movie crew.

"I bet they come in a truck," Stevie said.

"At least two," Lisa said. "Remember that woman's notebook?"

The woman she was referring to was the film's production manager. Max had spent two days with her right after he'd agreed to let them come to Pine Hollow. Her job was to figure out exactly what the company needed to bring and what was already here. She seemed very pleased after two days of hunting through every nook and cranny of the stable as well as the surrounding countryside. However, she had taken copious notes, and the girls were sure that every note in her notebook meant an item the company had to bring all the way from California.

When the movie crew finally showed up they had two trucks, not one, but they were rented from local movie companies and hadn't been shipped from California. In addition to the trucks, there were location vans and lots of cars filled with technical people.

"The way I see it, there are lights people, sound people, camera people, and then there are other people who just seem to run around, carrying things," Carole said.

"Those are the gofers," Stevie told her.

Carole looked at her quizzically.

"Yeah, you know, like go for coffee, go for donuts . . ."

Carole smiled. "Yeah, there are a lot of them. But where are the actors?"

"Anyone in particular?" Lisa teased.

"Aren't you girls supposed to be grooming the ponies now?" Max asked, approaching them from the rear.

They jumped in surprise. Of course, they were supposed to be grooming the ponies, but there was so much to see right where they were that they didn't want to leave.

"Aw, Max!" Stevie complained.

"A promise is a promise," Max said. "Otherwise . . ." He let his words hang like a threat. They would have tried to talk him out of making them work right then except that somebody wearing a set of headphones came running over to him with an urgent question having to do with water for coffee. Max was whisked into action.

"If Max has to become a gofer, the least we can do is groom the ponies," Carole conceded. "However, we don't have to do it indoors, do we? Why don't we groom them in the paddock next to the trucks so we can see everything while we work?"

It was a brilliant idea. It took only a minute to bring three ponies into the paddock and begin work.

The girls were fascinated with everything. All around them the large crew bustled away, hoisting things, moving things and measuring things. Nobody paid any attention to the three girls grooming the three ponies.

They became so engrossed with an argument between the headphone-wearer and somebody else that they didn't notice the arrival of six Winnebago vans. Skye Ransom emerged from one of them. He spotted his friends, all hanging on every word the assistant director said to the other man.

"You shouldn't eavesdrop on nasty conversations like that," he said, approaching them from behind.

The three girls turned to see their friend, and all interest in the nearby argument dropped instantly.

"Skye!" Lisa exclaimed, so excited that she dropped her curry comb. It hit the pony's foot and startled him so that he bolted away, yanking at the knot that secured him to the fence. The knot slipped, and the rope dropped from the fence. The pony started prancing around the paddock. The girls would have loved nothing better than to ignore the problem and chat with Skye, but horses came first.

"Be right back," Stevie said, excusing herself.

"Can I help?" Skye offered.

"No thanks," Carole told him.

It took them only a minute to catch the pony and bring him back to the fence, but it was long enough for Veronica diAngelo to seize an opportunity. Veronica was a spoiled rich girl who always seemed to think that only she was allowed to have good things happen to her.

"It's so wonderful you could join us here," Veronica cooed to Skye when The Saddle Club girls were busy trying to tie the pony's lead rope securely.

Skye looked a little confused. "Uh, thanks," he said awkwardly.

"Skye, this is Veronica diAngelo," Lisa said. Skye nodded politely. Then Lisa completed the introduction. "Veronica," she said. "This is Mr. Ransom."

Skye offered his hand. It was Veronica's turn to look confused. She had been outfoxed and she knew it. She didn't like it when she got outsnubbed. She shook Skye's hand and tried to smile. At the same time, The Saddle Club was trying *not* to smile.

"I have to go see to my purebred Arabian mare now," Veronica said. "I'll see you all later, maybe." She spoke through clenched teeth. Stevie, Lisa, and Carole loved every second of it.

"Who was *that?*" Skye asked, watching Veronica walk off.

The girls couldn't hold it anymore. They burst into giggles and, between waves of laughter, told Skye all about her.

"She thinks she owns everybody and everyone," Lisa said. "Uh, including you."

"I gathered that," Skye said. "She's in for a disappointment, though, because I am not a purebred Arabian mare type. I'm more the—here, let me show you. It's right in my trailer."

The girls looked at him quizzically, but saved their questions. First they had to finish grooming the ponies and take them back to their stalls. When that was done, they followed Skye to his trailer. He told them about the movie as they walked.

"It's about a boy named Gavin. He loves animals, especially his dog, Maverick, and his horse. Incidentally, that's a place where you are going to have to help me.

Can you choose a horse for me, Lisa? It's going to have to be a horse that will put up with me as a rider."

"You want me to choose your horse for the movie?" Lisa asked, surprised that he would trust her that much.

"I sure do," Skye said. "After all, you know exactly how poor a rider I am and what I need in a horse. You know it better than any coach I could bring in from the outside. Which horse do you recommend?"

Lisa thought for a minute as she and her friends walked across Pine Hollow's front lawn. She knew she could ask Carole and Stevie if they had any ideas, but Skye had wanted her opinion, not Stevie and Carole's. "I'm going to have to think about it for a bit. When do you first have to ride?" she asked.

"Not until after lunch. The assistant director wanted me to have a test ride before then. Could we do it?"

"Sure," Lisa said. "We can clear it with Max. I'm sure it will be okay." She looked at her watch. "We'll ride at eleven o'clock. That's in about forty-five minutes."

"Great," Skye said. "Now, prepare to meet my other co-star." With that, he turned the handle on his trailer and opened the door. He was greeted with an exuberant "Woof!"

The three girls followed Skye into the trailer. The source of the "woof" was a nondescript mutt with sandy-colored, curly hair and pointed ears that flopped over.

His tail wagged eagerly, and he stood up on his hind feet to give Skye a sloppy kiss. The whole scene melted the girls' hearts.

"The problem with this movie," Skye said with a grin, "is that every time Maverick is on the set, I'm upstaged. He's so adorable, he's going to steal the show."

"You could do worse than be upstaged by a perfectly charming mutt like this," Lisa said, patting Maverick as vigorously as she could. She had a dog of her own and loved all kinds of dogs, almost as much as she loved horses.

"But how am I going to explain it when he wins the Oscar and I have to accept it for him?"

The girls laughed, and then Stevie asked Skye to tell them what Maverick and the horse had to do with the story line.

"Oh, yes, I got distracted," he said. They all sat down in his spacious trailer to hear the rest of the story. "So, anyway, Gavin loves his horse and his dog. He's a real loner, and he's happy with things that way, until his dog loses a leg in a beaver trap and Gavin has to learn to trust the people who can help Maverick."

"Loses a leg! What are you going to do to Maverick?" Stevie blurted out. She was horrified.

"Oh, here, let me show you," Skye said. Then he turned to Maverick. "Leg, boy, *leg*," he said. He made a fist as he spoke. It seemed to be as much a signal to Maverick as the words had been. Maverick obediently stood up, tucked his right rear leg up next to his body, and walked on three legs.

"Unless you're looking right at it, you can hardly see his tucked-up leg. This dog is fantastic," Skye said.

"How did he learn that?" Carole asked.

"He was trained. He can do a lot of other tricks, too, but this is the most important for this movie. His trainer is here, too, and normally he would stay with the trainer, but I'm just crazy about him, and I thought it was important for us to get to know one another, so I asked if Maverick could stay in my trailer."

"You're really lucky," Lisa said to Skye. She sat on the floor next to Maverick and gave the deserving dog a big hug. Then she turned back to Skye. "Do you think Maverick would like to come along on our ride?"

Skye was about to answer that question, when Maverick answered for himself. He stood up—on all four legs—and barked loudly, wagging his tail. "We'll have to get permission to take him along, but it will probably be all right. After all, he's going to spend a lot of time with me *and* my horse while we're filming. We need to know that the horse and the dog get along!"

"Let's go, then," Carole said. Whenever a horseback ride was involved, she was eager. "I'll clear it with Max and meet you guys in the barn. What horse shall I tell him Skye is riding?" she asked Lisa.

Lisa knew the answer by then. "Pepper, of course," she said. Pepper was the horse she usually rode, and Lisa was very fond of the old, dappled gray. He was gentle and sensitive. He was also one of the older horses in the stable and had had lots of experience with inexperienced riders. She was certain Skye would like him.

"Good choice," Carole said. "They'll get along well."

"And Pepper's pretty, too. He'll be very photogenic," Stevie agreed.

"Then it's decided," Skye said. "Let's get going. The director is going to have to okay whatever horse I ride, so we can show him Pepper on our way to the trail."

Stevie and Carole went to tack up their horses. Lisa and Skye stayed together. Skye watched while Lisa put the tack on a chestnut gelding named Comanche, whom she would ride. She took Comanche to the paddock and secured him to the fence. Then she got Pepper's tack from the tack room. Skye helped her tack up Pepper. Maverick watched every move from where he stood outside the stall.

"You don't have to help," Lisa said to Skye.

"I know," Skye said. "But, see, people are always wanting to do things for me. I like to help."

"Okay, then, check to make sure the padding doesn't have any wrinkles in it on that side, please."

Skye confirmed that it was smooth, and very soon Lisa brought Pepper out to the paddock as well.

She was careful to notice that the tack was secure and Pepper was ready for mounting. She didn't notice that quite a few people from the movie company were standing nearby, adjusting lights and microphone booms. She'd become accustomed to the fact that whenever Skye was around, everybody was watching him.

She reminded Skye how to hold the reins while he was mounting the horse and held Pepper's bit steadily until she was sure Skye was securely in the saddle. She patted the horse's neck reassuringly.

"Now remember," she told Skye. "You're the boss. Pepper may be bigger than you are, but he's looking to you for leadership. If you don't take the lead, he will, and then you'll be in big trouble."

"This sounds familiar," Skye said, smiling at her. Pepper took a few steps forward.

"That's a cue to you," she said. "You didn't tell him to go forward, so now, make him go back to where he was. Pull gently on the reins."

Skye followed her instructions. Pepper returned to his original position and then stood peacefully.

"Congratulations," Lisa said to him. "You're now in charge."

She took Comanche's reins in her left hand and prepared to mount the horse.

"Nice job," a voice said from behind her. Lisa turned to see a middle-aged man in blue jeans and a polo shirt. He was walking toward her. "Are you going to introduce us?" the man asked Skye.

"Uh, Lisa, this is the director of the movie. His name is Oliver Mathews. Oliver, meet Lisa Atwood."

Lisa shook the man's hand politely.

"You handle the horses well," Oliver said. Lisa blushed a little bit.

"She's a great instructor, Oliver," Skye said. "In fact, she's the best teacher I ever had."

"Oh, come on," Lisa said. She hadn't done anything special at all. She'd just helped Skye into the saddle and given him a very small riding tip. She told the two of them as much.

"Maybe it doesn't seem like much to you," Oliver said, "but it was impressive to me. There is a very small part in this movie that we have to cast locally because the boy we cast got sick. It's a young boy who works in the stable where Gavin rides, but the part could just as well be played by a girl. There are only a few lines, and they're something like 'Want me to tack up Dixie for you?' Would you be interested in playing that part, Lisa?"

"Me?" she asked. She was so astonished at the question that she looked over her shoulders to see if there was another Lisa behind her that he was actually talking to.

"Yes, you," Oliver assured her. "You'd do very nicely, I'm sure."

"Of course she would," said a voice emerging from the stable. It was Stevie coming to her rescue. She walked right up to Oliver, leading her horse, Topside. "She'd be terrific and she'd be glad to do it. You're going to have to talk to her parents, though. Why don't you call them while we go on our little trail ride? Max has the number, or I can give it to you."

Stevie was talking as fast as she could before Lisa, who was still so astonished she could barely talk, said something else dumb.

"Yes, I'll do that," Oliver agreed. "You're her agent, I presume?" he teased.

"That's me," Stevie said, liking the joke. She offered her hand. "My name's Stevie Lake. I represent all the local stars. Let's do lunch sometime, okay?"

"Deal," Oliver said, shaking her hand. Then he waved to the riders. "Now, go on your trail ride and enjoy yourselves. I'm going to work Skye and Lisa hard later on, so have fun now."

Carole clicked her tongue at Starlight and nudged him gently in the belly to get him moving. The four riders headed for the trails behind Pine Hollow. Once the trail left the paddock, it doubled back, parallel to the stable. That gave Lisa, Stevie, and Carole the opportunity to watch Veronica, all decked out in her fanciest riding clothes, bring her horse out to the paddock for mounting, clearly hoping that Oliver would notice her great skill and beauty. It gave The Saddle Club no end of pleasure to see that her horse, Garnet, irritated by a wrinkle in his saddle pad, took a small hop while Veronica was in the process of mounting him. It was enough to land her, very unceremoniously, in the mud.

"I don't think that will get her a part in the movie," Stevie observed.

"Unless it's a slapstick comedy," Skye agreed.

Lisa couldn't remember a time when she'd been happier or more excited. She was only vaguely aware of the fact that she was riding a horse. It was more like flying. There she was, horseback riding with Skye Ransom, and she was actually going to be in a movie.

"Ready to trot?" Carole asked.

Lisa felt as if she were soaring already.

THE NEXT MORNING Lisa found things moving a little more slowly than they had on her ride with her friends and Skye the day before. In fact, things had been moving so fast the day before, Lisa's head was practically spinning. In the space of a few hours, she'd been "hired" to work for the rest of the week. She was actually going to be *paid* to work with Skye Ransom! Because she was under eighteen she had to have a chaperone on or around the set. Most young performers had their parents there. Skye had an uncle who traveled with him. Both of Lisa's parents worked and couldn't take the time off on such short notice. Max had agreed, somewhat reluctantly, to take the responsibility. He'd be around there anyway. Besides, if her parents had been around, they would have been so curious all the time Lisa was sure nothing would have gotten done.

Not that much was being done now. She had arrived on the set at six A.M. as she'd been instructed. She'd already memorized all of her lines, too. Once she had to say, "Your horse is ready, Gav." Another of her lines was "Beautiful dog!" Her third line was much easier. All she had to say was "Aww." Her fourth line was a simple "Thanks." It hadn't taken long to learn them.

At five after six that morning, she'd been whisked into the wardrobe and makeup trailers. She had worn her riding clothes to the set, and it took four adults looking over every inch of her to decide that her own riding clothes would do very nicely for her part. They did get somebody to polish her boots. He was able to make them shine. It didn't look right to Lisa.

"If you're hanging around a stable like my character does," she explained, "your boots don't usually shine this way. They get muddy and dirty."

"This is a film," the wardrobe mistress said rather sternly. "Not reality. People can see dirty boots anywhere. In a film like this, they want to see shiny boots."

There was no point in arguing. Lisa decided that maybe her character had just gotten a new pair of boots. That was reality and would explain the shiny boots.

Next, Lisa found herself in a tall chair in front of a mirror, having makeup applied. She liked the makeup woman a lot more than she had the wardrobe woman. The makeup woman had a better idea of reality.

"My name's Jeanette," she said. "I'm going to work my very hardest to make you look exactly like yourself. If I do that, then I've done my job," she explained.

Jeanette was chatty and friendly and seemed to sense Lisa's confusion and fears about being a part of the movie. She did everything she could to make Lisa relax and feel at ease. Jeanette told her she could talk as much as she wanted, except when she was working on Lisa's mouth. As Jeanette worked, Lisa told her all about The Saddle Club.

There were a lot of steps to the job of applying makeup to Lisa's face, but when it was done, Lisa agreed she looked pretty much like herself, except she was wearing a pale pink lipstick. Her mother rarely let her wear any lipstick at all, so it made her feel special to have it on.

"Off you go," Jeanette said, scooting Lisa out of the chair and welcoming her next actor.

"Where to?" Lisa asked.

"If you don't know the answer to that," Jeanette replied, "then the answer has to be school."

"School? I thought I was supposed to be in a movie." Lisa was confused.

"Of course you are, but until they need you on the set, you have to go to classes. Didn't they tell you that?"

Lisa shook her head. It was the first she'd heard of it. She had thought she was going to miss a whole week of school just so she could deliver her four lines. Now, it seemed, she was going to have to work *and* go to school.

"It's the law," Jeanette explained. "The AD's outside. Ask him where you're supposed to go. See you tomorrow, okay? And, uh, break a leg, Lisa." Jeanette waved gaily, and Lisa understood she was supposed to go. She just didn't know where. She opened the door and left the trailer. There were two people standing outside the trailer. One was a man, the other a boy about her own age.

It was totally overwhelming. Lisa had no idea what an AD was, and she couldn't imagine why a nice person like Jeanette was telling her to break her leg. This movie world was something else! She just hoped she didn't make a total fool of herself while she learned all about it.

"Hi, you must be Lisa," a man said, greeting her by the door. "My name's John. I'm the assistant director."

That answered Lisa's question about what an AD was. It stood for assistant director. Lisa shook his hand politely. Then he introduced her to the boy. His name was Jesse Macomber. John said Jesse was Skye's stand-in.

"You're due in class now. School sessions are taking

place in Mrs. Reg's office off the tack room. Do you know where that is?"

"Of course," she said.

"Good, then you can take Jesse here with you. He doesn't know where it is. We'll be needing you at about nine o'clock. We'll call for you then."

"Okay," Lisa agreed. She started to leave, but John stopped her.

"Oliver tells me you've never acted before, is that right?"

Lisa didn't like to admit it. It wasn't that she was ashamed. She was just afraid that if somebody found out she didn't have the slightest idea of what she was doing, they'd change their minds. Still, it was a direct question and she had to answer.

"It's true," she said.

John smiled warmly. "Well, then, break a leg, okay?"

Lisa glanced down at her legs. What was wrong with them that everybody kept talking about them?

John and Jesse laughed at her obvious confusion.

"I'll tell you what, Lisa," Jesse said. "You tell me what a tack room is, and I'll tell you why you're supposed to break your leg."

"This way," Lisa said, relieved. "You explain first."

"Break a leg has to do with an old performers' superstition," Jesse said. "See, when actors go on stage, there is

38

always the risk that something awful could happen that would mess up the show or be embarrassing. It's every performer's nightmare. We try to think about the worst possible thing that could happen, knowing that whatever we're prepared for is exactly the thing that won't happen."

"I get it," Lisa said, sort of understanding. "If you tell somebody to break their leg, then they won't break their leg and the performance will go smoothly."

"Right," Jesse said. "Now tell me about tack rooms."

Lisa was in her element. She was glad to be able to talk about something familiar. She told Jesse all about tack and was in the middle of comparing jumping and dressage saddles by the time they walked through the tack room and into Mrs. Reg's office, which had been converted into a classroom. She had also learned some things from Jesse. Jesse was Skye's stand-in, meaning that when Skye wasn't being filmed, Jesse was often used on the set to check things like camera angles and lighting. One day Jesse hoped to be an actor himself, he told Lisa, but for now he was glad to have the work.

Lisa realized then that, to a lot of the people around the set, movie-making was work. It wasn't a lark and an opportunity to have a week off from regular school. It was a job.

Lisa had learned many things in Mrs. Reg's office at Pine Hollow since she'd begun riding there, but never had she learned earth science there. It was quite a switch for her to be surrounded by saddles and bridles and to be studying school subjects. There was one tutor named Sabina for all the youngsters working on the movie. At first just Lisa and Jesse were there. Skye was working on a scene, and Lisa was scheduled to begin rehearsal in twenty minutes. The tutor didn't waste any time. Right away she had Lisa begin a chart, locating earthquake epicenters. It surprised Lisa to find that she actually learned something in those twenty minutes.

Then the AD, John, called for her and brought her to where her first scene was to be shot. The scene was quite a long one, but her part was only a small bit of it. On a cue from John, she was supposed to lead Pepper out of the stable and hold the reins while Skye mounted up.

She did as she was told, uttering the immortal line, "Your horse is ready, Gav," as she did so.

"Cut, print, thank you," the director said. That was it. She was done. The scene was over.

Lisa had read enough about movies to know that most scenes had to be shot at least a couple of times before it was done right. She smiled to herself, proud that her own scene had been done right the first time.

"I can go now?" she asked John.

At first he looked surprised. Then he laughed. "No," he said. "There are a few more things to do."

It turned out that there were a *lot* more things to do.

What they had shot the first time was sort of a master. Lisa was right that it had been done well the first time and that was good. What she didn't realize was that they then wanted to get a number of angles of the same scene so the editor would have a few choices when the final scene was assembled.

Lisa never had to speak her brilliant line again, but she certainly had to go through the motions of the scene again. Most of the retakes concentrated on Skye. There were close-ups on his face and his hands. They filmed him from every angle climbing into the saddle.

Then the cameras turned to Lisa and Pepper. They were filmed walking together, standing together, even trotting together. The camera followed Lisa's hands and then her feet. There was even a shot taken from a dog's point of view of the whole scene.

Although the actions were incredibly repetitive, Lisa was fascinated by it all and never even looked at her watch. When Oliver announced that it was time for lunch, she was very surprised to find that it was already one o'clock.

Skye and Lisa took sandwiches and soda from the buffet table and practically wolfed them down.

"I don't know why I'm so hungry," Lisa said, embarrassed by how much she was eating.

"It's because you're working hard," Skye said. "And

soon you're going to have to work even harder. See, we've got to get back to school now."

"Again?"

"You were there for just twenty minutes this morning, weren't you? You've got to put in a lot more time to satisfy the law. And I heard Oliver say they want to redo a couple of those close-ups on you and on me."

Lisa started laughing. Skye was a little surprised. "I don't need to go to school to learn," she explained. "I've learned more here in a couple of hours than I would have thought possible. I've learned that all the people here, including the children, are doing a job. I've also learned that the job is often tedious and hard work. If anybody ever tries to tell me that movie acting is a glamour business, I'll set them straight, okay?"

"Deal," Skye said, shaking her hand. "Now, let's get to class before the tutor sends out the dogs for us."

The afternoon session at school was interesting, too. Lisa did some more work on earthquakes, and then all four of the students there had a spelling bee. Spelling was one of Lisa's strengths. She beat everybody else with the word "picnicking." Jesse and Skye congratulated her. So did Alicia, the stand-in for the girl who played Gavin's sister. Jesse and Skye sounded as if they meant it. Alicia didn't. Lisa wasn't sorry when John called Alicia to the set.

At three o'clock school was dismissed. According to the schedule that was posted, Lisa was supposed to be done for the day at three-thirty. That suited her well because Stevie and Carole were coming over to Pine Hollow straight from school to do their hour of stable work for Max, and then the three of them were going to the mall to buy things for Colonel Hanson's birthday party.

When three-thirty came, however, Lisa found herself back on the set. Oliver and John told Lisa and Skye that they'd checked the first prints of the scene they'd shot in the morning, and the lighting was all wrong. They had misjudged the strength of the natural light. They had to shoot the whole scene completely over.

Everybody was grumbling about the mistake. Lisa remembered the argument Oliver had had earlier and wondered if it was connected.

"This better not happen again," John growled, frowning at the lighting crew.

Lisa raised her hand until Oliver noticed her. "I think I know something that will help," she said. Everyone turned to listen, wondering what this newest member of the cast could come up with. "It's a Pine Hollow tradition," she explained. "And it's right here." She pointed to the doorway where Skye was to mount Pepper. "We call it the good-luck horseshoe. All the Pine Hollow riders touch it before we begin a ride. Nobody who has touched it has ever been seriously hurt in a riding accident. I'm pretty sure it would cover film crews, too. Want to try?"

There was a heavy moment of silence. It was broken by a burst of laughter from Oliver and John. Then the rest of the crew joined in.

"It's certainly worth a try!" Oliver agreed. He was the first to touch the horseshoe. After Oliver touched it, everybody else there, including the cameramen, lined up to do the same.

Stevie and Carole arrived as the chief electrician was touching the horseshoe. They waved wildly at Lisa and both started talking at once.

"Are you wearing *lipstick?*" Stevie asked.

"Why's everyone touching the horseshoe?" Carole asked.

"Yes I am, and I thought everybody was going to come to blows about the lights, so I wanted to try to change the mood," answered Lisa.

"Well, everybody's laughing now," Carole said. "So you must be some sort of genius."

"Oh, she is," Skye chimed in, fresh from the good-luck horseshoe himself. "Why didn't you tell me she could spell everything? She showed the rest of us up in a spelling bee!" He gave Lisa a little hug around her shoulders.

"We want to hear it all," Stevie said seriously.

"You will. I promise," Lisa said.

"How long until you can leave so we can go to the mall?" Stevie asked. "We're going to go to TD's first."

Lisa looked at her watch again. It was three-thirty. She wanted to go to the ice-cream parlor and the mall with her friends, but the crew was going to reshoot everything they had done in the morning. It would take at least a couple of hours. She'd been looking forward to an impromptu Saddle Club meeting, but she wasn't going to have it today.

"I can't," she said. "The goof they made is going to keep me here until dark. Can we do it tomorrow?"

"No, because I've already made a deal with Dad to meet us at the mall at six," Carole said. "I can't reach him to change that, so we have to go now."

"Oh, I'm sorry," Lisa said. She felt awful about it. She'd been looking forward to spending time with her friends, planning the colonel's party.

"Look, what you're doing now is once in a lifetime, and never for most people. Don't worry. We can get lots done by ourselves," Carole reassured her.

"Talk to you later, okay?" Stevie said.

"Deal," Lisa said.

"Places!" Oliver announced. It was time to get back to work.

Stevie and Carole headed for the stable, where they were going to muck out stalls. Lisa returned to her place on the movie set.

5

"WHERE DO WE go first when we get to the mall?" Carole asked Stevie after they had settled into a booth at TD's and placed their orders.

Stevie's mind was on something else. She was thinking about Lisa and the movie set. Stevie and Carole had taken a few minutes from mucking out stables to watch the filming. "Wasn't Lisa just wonderful?" Stevie asked. "I mean, the way she did just what the director told her to do and Pepper looked so great. It was fabulous, wasn't it?"

"Yeah, it was," Carole agreed. "Although I didn't like the fact that Pepper had been working such long hours. He's not young anymore, you know." It was just like Carole to think about the long hours that Pepper was working and not think about the long hours that Lisa and Skye were working.

"He was just walking back and forth coming out the door of the stable," Stevie reminded her.

"But all those times Skye mounted him. That can be quite difficult on a horse."

"To say nothing of how difficult that can be on Skye," Stevie said pointedly.

"I guess so," Carole admitted, "but a horse doesn't get paid a lot of money, and he can't complain when something bothers him."

"Maybe," Stevie agreed. "Except that it seems to me that over the years horses have developed pretty good ways of complaining when they think they've worked enough. Like when they race for the stable the minute they decide their ride is over?"

Carole smiled. It was true. Horses did usually move faster going back to the barn than away from it.

"And, uh, speaking of going places, where are we going at the mall?" Carole asked, bringing the conversation back to the main topic of the afternoon.

"I saw in this week's paper that there's a sale at Marie's," Stevie told her.

"Marie's is a dress shop," Carole said. "Is that what you propose to buy for my father for his birthday? Because if you do, I think he and some of his Marine Corps buddies may have a few things to say about it."

"No, no," Stevie said. "I was just thinking that, as long as we're out there—you know. We might look for something for us, like to wear to the party."

Carole dug into her sundae, which had just arrived. "I was thinking more of getting some plates or something."

"Plates?" Stevie asked. She was so surprised she couldn't even pick up her spoon. "What do we want with plates?"

"Well, for, like to eat off of," Carole explained.

"Don't you already have some of those in your house? I mean, seems to me the last time I ate there, we definitely used plates. I think they had flowers on them. Did they all break?"

"Of course not," said Carole. "But don't you think we should use paper plates for the party?"

"Okay, then, we'll use paper plates," Stevie agreed. "Then we won't have so much to clean up. Good thinking."

"But what are we going to put on them?" Carole asked. "If we're giving a party, we have to have food and things to drink, don't we?"

"Every good party does," Stevie agreed. "The trouble

is, I don't have any idea what to get—or how much. Do you know how many people are coming?"

Carole shook her head. "We sent out the invitations a while ago, and some people have called or told me in person that they were coming, but I don't remember who or how many."

"Some party-giving team we are," Stevie said, almost groaning. "We need to organize."

"We sure do. The problem is that we've always been able to rely on Lisa to do the organizing, but she's busy with Skye and the movie."

Stevie put her chin in her cupped hands and her elbows on the table. It was a way she had of thinking. There was no doubt about it: Lisa, the straight-A student, was the organizer of the group. She could always figure out what needed to be done. Stevie was the one who then usually figured out how to get it done. Without Lisa, she felt a little lost.

"Darn that movie," Stevie said. "It's ruining the party."

"Nah," Carole said. "It's just making it harder. Besides, it's a wonderful thing for Lisa. Even though we miss her for this, what she's doing is important."

"I know, I know," said Stevie. "I just wish—"

"Yeah, me too," Carole agreed.

"All right, then, but what is, is. So, let's get started on our own. Let's make a list."

That seemed like a very good idea until both girls realized that neither of them had either paper or pencil to make it with. Fortunately, the waitress loaned them an order pad and a dull pencil. It was a start.

Their first stop at the mall was Marie's, where, as Stevie predicted, there was a sale going on. They didn't have enough money to buy anything, even on sale, but that didn't stop them from trying on clothes.

"Isn't this pink top just beautiful?" Carole asked, holding it up to herself in front of a mirror.

"Very pretty," Stevie agreed. "And I bet it would go well with your green skirt. You could wear that to the party. Your dad would love it!"

"Oh, the party," Carole said, recalling their actual mission at the mall. "I think we'd better get going, don't you?"

Reluctantly, the girls left Marie's and moved on to another store. Their next stop was a joke shop. Stevie was in seventh heaven. The place was filled with things that made strange sounds and/or jumped out of containers at unexpected moments. There was even a battery-operated "human" hand that sort of wiggled.

"Oh, gross!" Carole said.

"Your dad would love it!" Stevie said.

"That's what I meant," said Carole. "Anyway, we're not here to buy a present for Dad. The party *is* his present. We're supposed to be buying things for the party, and I don't think a wiggling rubber 'hand' is exactly what we need to make the party a success."

"Yeah," Stevie agreed reluctantly. "Let's try another place, okay?"

Over the next hour and a half, the girls felt as though they went into every single store in the whole mall. They paused only briefly in the shoe shops and the earring stalls, but they closely scrutinized everything for sale in the sporting goods shops—especially the riding equipment—and in the men's clothing store. Nothing seemed at all right for Colonel Hanson's party.

As Carole and Stevie walked through the mall, they window-shopped, draped scarves on themselves, practiced swinging golf clubs, admired shoes, and ate fudge samples. They saw some friends from Pine Hollow and chatted about the excitement of the movie-making at the stable. The one thing they didn't do was purchase anything for Colonel Hanson's party.

Every few minutes Stevie went fishing in her purse and pulled out the now-tattered piece of paper with their "list." It didn't help much. All it said was "party supplies" and "plates."

Stevie looked at Carole's watch. They had only ten minutes until they were supposed to meet Carole's father in the parking lot of the mall for their ride home. "I know!" she said. "We can get plates at the party-supply section of the variety store." She grabbed Carole's hand, said "Follow me," and dragged her through the door.

The two of them went right past penny candy, stockings, hair rollers, bows, even barrettes, and made their way right through stationery, not even pausing to look at ballpoint pens or five-millimeter mechanical pencils.

"Here they are!" Stevie declared. There, in front of the two of them, was a positively amazing array of paper plates for birthday parties. For a moment it seemed that they might actually be able to purchase something on their shopping list. However, closer inspection revealed that the selection at this shop was strictly limited to Saturday-morning cartoon characters.

"This doesn't look quite right to me," Carole said.

"But didn't I hear your father talking the other day about how much he loved Michelangelo?" Stevie asked, hoping desperately that they'd be able to buy at least *something* for the party.

"A different Michelangelo," replied Carole. "The one dad likes was the sculptor and painter—not a turtle."

"Oh," Stevie said. "Well, I don't think there's a line of paper plates with the Sistine Chapel on it, so let's forget it. It's time to meet your dad now, anyway."

Carole looked at her watch and agreed. "We didn't get much done, did we?"

"Not much," Stevie said. "But we did have fun. Anyway, we can come again. Maybe Lisa can come with us next time."

"I hope so," Carole said, opening the door that led to the parking lot. "It may be that Hollywood needs Lisa, but it's clear that we need her more!"

Colonel Hanson honked to get the girls' attention. They ran over to the car and climbed into the backseat.

"Ah, making me feel like a chauffeur," he teased. "Well, then, where to, mademoiselles?"

"Home, Jeeves," Stevie commanded.

The colonel turned the car around and headed back toward Willow Creek. "So tell me," he said, speaking over his shoulder to his passengers in the back. "What did you two accomplish at the mall this afternoon?"

"Nothing," they answered in a single voice, more than a little aware of how true that was.

SKYE AND LISA perched on a paddock fence, watching Samson trot happily in circles. They chatted easily while Oliver and the rest of the crew considered whether there was enough light left to do any more filming for the day.

"As a matter of fact, I was right here when you called the other day," Lisa said. "I was working with Stevie and Carole on Samson's training. He's supposed to be getting used to a bit now. He doesn't like it much, but he's a good sport about it."

"You three have an awful lot of fun together, don't you?" Skye asked suddenly.

"Of course," Lisa answered, surprised by the question. "We do everything together—at least everything our parents will let us. Sometimes it's trouble, but it's just about always fun. What kinds of things do you do with your friends?"

"Not much," Skye said. He seemed embarrassed to be admitting it. "For one thing, I don't have many friends. I'm working on movies most of the time, which means I'm not in regular school. The other kids I work with have the same kind of schedule I do, and that means there isn't much time for fun."

"But what about weekends and vacations and things?" Lisa asked.

"Sure, I have time off, but the fact is that it's very hard for me to go out and do the 'normal' stuff that you and Carole and Stevie do. Wherever I go, people are bugging me. They don't mean it in any bad way. Most of them feel as if they know me because they saw me in one movie or another, but they don't know *me*, they just know the character I played."

"Does it make you angry?" Lisa asked, realizing for the first time that the life of a star might not be one hundred percent wonderful.

"Not anymore. It just makes it hard. Sometimes I wish I could just be me and do the things I want when I want to, not because my agent or my producer says I have to."

"But the things you have to do are so exciting, and the things I get to do are so boring!" Lisa said.

"I think boring can be fun," Skye said. "For instance, after we wrap here for the night, I'm supposed to go back to the motel with my chaperone. We'll order dinner in. I'll study my lines and go to bed. That's all."

"Want to do something more boring?" Lisa asked.

"You have any suggestions?"

"Well, I could show you around Willow Creek. Now that's boring!"

"Let's do it!" Skye said. Lisa couldn't believe how excited he seemed by the prospect.

A few minutes later, Oliver told everybody they could go. Lisa went back to the makeup trailer to have her makeup taken off. Skye said he'd meet her in front of the stable. It took almost half an hour before Skye showed up. He apologized and explained that he'd had to get permission from three different people to take a little walk around Willow Creek with her. However, they had all agreed, and that was the important part.

Skye offered Lisa his arm and they were off.

"Any tour of Willow Creek begins with the center of all activity here," said Lisa. "It's a place known as TD's. That stands for Tastee Delight, and that is where I am going to buy you an ice-cream sundae."

They walked together toward the shopping center where TD's was located.

"I meant to ask you where Stevie and Carole were

going this afternoon. You seemed disappointed not to be able to go with them."

"I hoped nobody noticed," Lisa said. "I was disappointed, but it seemed like such a silly thing. See, they were going to the mall to buy things for Colonel Hanson's surprise birthday party."

Skye's eyes lit up. "Oh, that sounds great! I bet Carole's dad is going to love it."

"I'm sure he is, even if we don't come up with something clever and wonderful to do at the party." Then Lisa had an idea. "Don't you go to a lot of parties in Hollywood where people are forever doing clever things that get written up in magazines? Do you have any suggestions for us?"

"Hmmm," Skye said thoughtfully. "Well, there was one party where somebody had their swimming pool filled with champagne. . . ."

"But then you couldn't swim!" Lisa said, quite horrified. She loved to swim.

"Exactly," Skye said. "I hated the party, but it *did* get written up in a magazine. Then there was another party I got invited to where the host flew everybody on a couple of jets to his mountaintop hideaway in the Rockies. . . ."

"I think that's a little beyond our budget," Lisa said woefully.

"It wasn't any fun anyway," Skye said. "Most of the

people there were more concerned with the fact that they had been invited to this exclusive party than with the idea of having fun. It was awful. Besides, the studio made me go with my co-star as a date, and she was a real pain."

"Is all this your way of telling me that these fancy Hollywood parties aren't any fun?" Lisa said, now disillusioned.

"Not really. Sometimes they are fun. But to tell you the truth, when I think of fun birthday parties, I think of the ones I used to go to before I became an actor. I think of games and balloons and, best of all, magicians. Now, in my opinion, a good magician *makes* a birthday party."

"Maybe, but do you think that's right for a man who is turning forty? Besides, a magician is a little out of our budget, too. All we can really do is get some good snacks, cook a few things, make a tasty punch, and put up some decorations. Believe me, Colonel Hanson is a terrific man. If we could afford it, we'd fly him and all his friends to a mountaintop hideaway in the Rockies."

Skye laughed and then smiled at Lisa. It was a smile Lisa had seen a dozen times on the screen and one that made most teenage girls—including Lisa Atwood—positively melt and swoon. In person, however, it didn't have the knee-melting quality that millions of girls adored. It was the warm and genuine smile of a warm and genuine friend. Lisa smiled back.

"This," she gestured grandly at the motley collection of shops in front of her, "is Willow Creek's shopping center. As you can see, we have two shoe stores, a supermarket, a liquor store, one jewelry shop—we used to have something they called a health spa, but it got sick and went out of business—and, most important, TD's. Come, be my guest!"

"I'd be charmed," Skye said. He followed her into the ice-cream shop.

It was after six o'clock, and only a few patrons were in TD's. Lisa took Skye over to The Saddle Club's favorite booth, the one in the far corner. One of Lisa's friends from school, Eloise Marshall, was at the counter, buying a quart of ice cream to take out. She came over to the table and said hello to Lisa and Skye. Lisa introduced her to Skye, though it was obvious that Eloise knew who Skye was.

"You missed a history test today," Eloise said.

That struck Lisa as odd. "You and I aren't in the same history section," Lisa reminded Eloise. "We had our test last week."

"Oh," Eloise said, and then blushed a deep pink. "Well, see you around," she stammered. "Nice to meet you, uh . . . Skye." The final word fairly oozed out of Eloise's mouth before the girl fled from TD's, leaving her change on the counter.

"I wonder what's the matter with her?" Lisa mused.

"It's me," Skye said. "Sometimes I have that effect on the most normal people."

"And, to be sure, Eloise is the most normal person you'll ever want to meet. Oh, well. What would you like? The ice cream is wonderful, and so are all the toppings. Trust me. I've tried every one of them."

"Hi, Lisa," the waitress said. Lisa hadn't known that she knew her name. "Your friends were here before. They looked lonely without you, but I can see you were busy." She smiled brightly. Lisa had never seen her behave this way. Usually she wasn't the least bit friendly. "What'll it be?"

"Hot fudge on vanilla for me," Lisa said.

"Me, too," Skye agreed.

"We've got a special on extra toppings," the waitress went on. "Walnuts or almonds are free today for good customers. We'll toss in a maraschino cherry, too."

"Almonds, no cherry," Skye said.

The waitress jotted a note to herself and walked away before she could even hear that Lisa didn't want anything extra.

"I'm beginning to see your problem," Lisa said as she watched the waitress wander away.

"The trouble is that it becomes *your* problem when you're around me," he said.

"I don't mind. I'm just surprised the way some people are transformed by somebody famous."

"You never were awed by me, were you?" Skye asked.

"Of course I was," Lisa said. "But remember, the first time I met you, you had just been thrown from a horse and you needed my help."

"How could I forget?" Skye asked. "There you were, a knight in shining armor—come to my rescue!"

"Hi, Lisa!" A warm greeting interrupted her conversation with Skye. Lisa looked up. It was Melanie Winkler. She was a classmate of Lisa's, and she was Eloise's best friend. She was also a health-food nut, and her diet did *not* include ice cream. Lisa knew immediately that she hadn't just dropped into TD's to pick up some ice cream for the family dessert.

Lisa introduced her to Skye. Melanie, it turned out, had seen every movie Skye had been in, and she wanted to talk about all of them with him. She also just happened to be carrying her favorite Skye Ransom poster, and would it be possible for him to autograph it?

Skye thanked her for her interest in his career, autographed the poster, and waited for her to leave. She didn't move. By then, she almost couldn't because she'd been joined by four other friends who just "happened" to be stopping by for a cone or a quart or to order an ice-cream cake. They all also just happened to have something Skye could autograph. He willingly signed his name for all of them. Then, although Lisa could hardly believe it when she thought about it later, one of the girls actually reached over and took Skye's water glass.

"I have his fingerprints, girls!" she shrieked, and then ran from the restaurant, sloshing water with every step.

"I think it's time for us to leave now," Lisa said. Skye nodded and they both started to stand up.

"Oh, you want him all to yourself," one of the girls said. "We're not good enough for you now that you've gone *Hollywood!*"

It wasn't a true or fair thing to say, and it made Lisa very angry. She was not the one who was behaving badly. It was her schoolmates, and she intended to give them a piece of her mind when the movie was finished. For now, all she wanted to do was get out of TD's.

Quickly Lisa fished into her wallet and put enough money on the table to cover the sundaes they'd never eat. Then she and Skye had to push through the crowd to get to the door, where they were greeted by an arriving horde of six more girls.

"There he *is!*" two of them shrieked at once. Girls Lisa had once thought of as her friends started running toward her and Skye in an uncontrolled frenzy.

Lisa panicked. How were they ever going to get out of this mess, and how could she have gotten Skye into it?

"This way!" Skye said urgently, taking her hand. The two of them moved quickly, almost running down the steps and out the door, and within a short time Lisa found herself following Skye into the backseat of a limousine that was magically waiting for them. The door closed firmly and the locks snapped protectively, shielding the two of them from a fast-growing crowd. Majestically the limousine pulled out of the shopping-center parking lot and turned onto the main road.

"Where did *this* come from?" Lisa asked, looking around her.

"It was Oliver's condition," Skye explained, a little embarrassed. "He said we could walk around, but that the car had to be there in case we needed it. He suspected this might happen."

"Wasn't that nice of him," Lisa said.

"Nice wasn't what motivated him," Skye explained. "He can't afford to have anything happen to me. Any delay in production would cost a bundle."

"Oh," Lisa said. "Your world is totally turned upside down, isn't it?"

"Yes. Definitely. That's one of the reasons I like being with you and your friends—uh, Carole and Stevie, I mean, not those guys." He gestured out the window. "Your world isn't upside down at all. It's just the way it ought to be."

"I always thought my world and my friends were pretty normal," Lisa said, "but when I saw Caitlin take your water glass and announce she had your fingerprints—well, I don't know anymore!"

Skye laughed. "That was a new one, I have to admit it. It's going to cramp my style, too. I *was* planning some daring daylight robberies of local establishments, but now that my fingerprints are on file . . ."

A silly image flashed in Lisa's mind. It was a picture of Skye, dressed as a cat burglar all in black, mounting the rose trellis of a local house. He was being followed by forty screaming teenage girls. She told Skye about her mental picture, and they both agreed it would make a career change to cat burglary very tough.

The limousine pulled into the driveway of Lisa's house and drew to a stop.

"I'll see you tomorrow," Lisa said to Skye. "Thanks for the lift. But I'm really sorry about what happened. It was awful, and I should have realized—"

"Don't worry," Skye said. "It was worth a try. Living normally is always worth a try. Thank you."

The chauffeur opened the door for Lisa, and she walked into her house. Movie sets, dressing rooms, special classes, and limousines were fun, but home was best and she was glad to be there. The limousine was gone by the time she turned for a final wave.

LISA TRIED TO answer all of her parents' questions about her day on the set, but what she really wanted to do was get to the phone and call Stevie. Parents were okay and hers were better than most, but what she needed was a friend. Besides, she was dying to hear about all the wonderful things Stevie and Carole had found at the mall.

Lisa's parents persisted.

"You mean you really got everybody working there to touch that dirty horseshoe?" her mother asked.

"I did, and it worked," Lisa said. "It made everybody laugh."

"So, just exactly what did you learn in the so-called school today?" her father asked.

"Earthquakes, for one thing," Lisa said. "I learned how to figure out where the epicenter is."

"Well, that's certainly an important thing for those Californians to know," her father said. "After all, the entire state could end up in the Pacific because of an earthquake. No wonder you spent the whole day studying earthquakes."

"Uh, Dad, the tutor was from Virginia, not California, and we spent class time on a lot of different things. For instance, I won the spelling bee. I also worked on math. The tutor showed me how to figure out square roots. My regular math teacher said it was one of those things you should use a calculator to do."

"Well, the tutor was right," her father said, conceding the point. "You should know how to do all those functions mathematically and then check your work on a calculator."

"And did you get to meet any *stars* in the movie?" her mother asked.

"How about Skye Ransom?" Lisa asked. "I spent a lot of time with him."

"No, I mean *real* stars," her mother said. Lisa knew that what she meant was adult stars. Mrs. Atwood didn't consider a teenager—even a multimillionaire teenager—a *star*.

"Mom, Skye *is* the star of the movie. Nobody else in it is as famous as he is." She was tired of the questions and wanted to talk to Stevie. "Look, I've got to study my lines for tomorrow, okay? And I've also got some homework to do. I'll see you later, okay?"

Before her parents could object, she headed for the stairs and the privacy of her room. She settled in comfortably on her bed and reached for the phone on her bedside table. The tutor hadn't assigned any homework, and the line she was going to have to memorize for the next day was securely in her memory. Although Lisa wasn't certain whether they'd be working on the "Beautiful dog!" scene or the "Aww!" one—she was pretty sure she didn't need to do any further memory work on either one.

"Stevie? It's Lisa," she said when her friend picked up the phone.

"Oh, how are you? How was it? Tell me everything you couldn't say when Skye was there!" Stevie said, sputtering questions at an amazing rate—amazing, that was, for anybody but Stevie.

"I'm fine. It was fun, and interesting and incredibly boring, and exciting all at the same time. I'll tell you everything, but first of all, I'm so sorry that I couldn't come along with you guys to the mall. What happened? What did you do?"

Stevie was more than a little surprised that Lisa would even care at all what had happened at the mall this afternoon, and she was embarrassed that they accomplished so little. "Well, nothing, really," she said quite truthfully. "Now, tell me about Skye and the life of a glamorous star."

"Did you buy anything for the party? I sort of worked out a list last night and I meant to give it to you and Carole because I thought it might help a little, but everything was so crazy when you got to the set—I mean Pine Hollow—that I just forgot. Did you make a list?"

Stevie had always known that Lisa was superconsiderate and superorganized, but this was beyond super. She just couldn't believe Lisa was actually worried about the party when she was working so hard all day long on a movie starring Skye Ransom.

"Come on, Lisa," Stevie said. "You don't have to worry about the party. You have to worry about being a Hollywood star. That's much more glamorous and important than a few hours that Carole and I wasted at the mall. Carole and I can handle this without you."

Lisa was surprised by what she was hearing from her friend, but she decided it was just Stevie's curiosity. "I took Skye to TD's," she began.

"I heard," Stevie told her. "Three people called me and told me about it. It must have been awful!"

"It was," Lisa agreed. "The worst part of it, aside from watching some people I thought I knew well behave like total idiots, was seeing how they thought that I had somehow changed—that I wasn't myself anymore." Lisa paused and then went on. "I'd hate to think that some people I do know well might feel that way, too."

Stevie got the message right away. "You mean you really do care what we got done at the mall?" she asked.

"Yes, I do. I want Colonel Hanson's party to be perfect. I promised to help you guys work on it, and I didn't like finking on the promise. So, tell me, what did you get done?"

Stevie sighed deeply. "Not much. We missed you and we needed your list and your organizational skills. We tried on dresses and earrings. We listened to a few tapes. We even looked at paper plates. But we didn't accomplish anything. I don't know how we're going to put together a party for the colonel on Saturday."

"Now I feel better," Lisa said.

"Because you were missed?" Stevie asked.

"Partly. But mostly because you're going to have to try to go shopping again and this time I can come along. That's what makes me feel better."

"Ah, the joys of having your cake and eating it, too!" Stevie said wistfully.

"Speaking of which, what kind of cake are we going to make for Carole's dad?" Lisa asked.

"Make? You think we're going to make a cake? Like with batter and an oven?"

Lisa recalled a number of adventures in cooking that she'd had with Stevie and Carole. One in particular had ended with a lot of gingerbread batter on the window of Stevie's kitchen. Another had produced pancakes—instead of a layer cake. Those were fun times, with a lot of laughs, to say nothing of cleanup, but perhaps it wasn't a good idea to take risks with the colonel's birthday cake.

"How about an ice-cream cake from TD's?" Lisa suggested.

The two of them had a good, long discussion about TD's ice-cream cake versus the bakery's almond torte, topped by TD's toasted almond ice cream. They didn't want to make a decision without Carole, but they did take the time to discuss all the advantages of each. Lisa's mouth was positively watering by the time they moved onto possible decoration schemes.

Eventually, the conversation turned back to Pine Hollow. Lisa told Stevie every detail of her day on the set—from Jeanette in makeup to Jesse's explanation of "break a leg." She told her about school and rehearsal and the lights and the director. She talked about how there was so much waiting and then, how it was all over in a few seconds—until they had to do it again! She talked very fast, the words fairly tumbling from her lips, but Stevie listened to every bit of it.

". . . and then there was the incident at TD's," Lisa

said. "The only good part about that was escaping in the limousine."

"Limousine? *Tell* me," Stevie urged her. So Lisa did.

When almost every minute of the day had been covered and Stevie's curiosity had been satisfied, she told Lisa to call Carole and repeat it all. Lisa said she would. Stevie promised her that she and Carole would schedule another trip to the mall. They would come over to Pine Hollow after school, and this time they would all go to the mall—no matter what time Oliver let her leave.

Later, after talking with Carole for a satisfying half hour, Lisa scrunched down on her bed and looked at the ceiling of her room, enjoying the quiet. She thought about herself and the girl she had been yesterday—just plain Lisa. She wondered how being in a movie with Skye Ransom had changed her. Then, when she thought about her two best friends, she understood that one of the nicest things about being friends with Stevie and Carole was that, no matter what happened, she was still just plain Lisa. On that thought, she fell asleep, exhausted.

"UP ALL NIGHT practicing your lines?" Skye asked when they met in makeup early one morning later in the week. This was the last scheduled day of shooting. Lisa was a little sad, and a little happy to think that it was all going to be over soon.

"'Aww'," Lisa said. "Or is it 'Beautiful dog!'"

"I think you did 'Aww' yesterday, along with 'Thank you'; it's 'Beautiful dog!' today."

"Stop talking or I'll put on the wrong shade of pancake and make your lips crooked," Jeanette said.

"You have to watch out for her," Skye told Lisa, almost seriously. "She spent years doing the makeup for horror films. She'll have hair sprouting out of your cheekbones in an instant!"

Jeanette grinned mischievously. "Do you want it curly or straight?" she asked.

"Curly. And I want pointy ears like Mr. Spock, too," Lisa said.

"Hmmmm," Jeanette mused, working hard to make Lisa look exactly the way she had looked the day before, and every other day of her life.

Then, while Jeanette put down her pencils and brushes to examine her subject, Lisa dared to speak again. "How come I'm admiring your dog today—as in 'Beautiful dog!'—when I already saw him in the scene we shot the first day?" she asked Skye. "I mean, shouldn't I have remarked on Maverick's beauty before instead of saying, 'Your horse is ready, Gav'?"

Skye smiled. "Seems that way, but remember, this is a movie. Although everybody who sees the movie will see you admire Maverick before you deliver my horse, we don't necessarily shoot the scenes in the order in which they happen. Shooting a movie isn't like performing a play. Everything is done in the most economical order, not the most sensible order. See, the filming is planned so that all the scenes that can be done in one place at one time are done at once. Also, they take into consideration who is in each scene. I'm scheduled for filming for these two weeks and then for another two weeks later next month. They don't want me sitting around, going to classes and collecting a salary for a minute more than they need me. It's all very complicated."

"And fascinating," Lisa said. "I hadn't thought about filming in those terms, but, of course, it makes sense. It's sort of like—"

"Shhh," Jeanette said. "I'm about ready to do the hair sprouting out of your cheekbones."

Lisa sat absolutely still while Jeanette finished her makeup. Once again Jeanette had succeeded in making her look exactly like herself. She noticed that Jeanette followed a chart she'd prepared the first day so Lisa's makeup would be identical from day to day. There was a lot that went on behind the scenes of movie-making that was completely invisible to moviegoers. Lisa liked getting the inside view of it all.

It turned out that the scene they were to shoot called for Skye to canter up toward the stable with Maverick following him. Lisa's job was to walk through the back door, take his reins, and kneel down to be greeted by Maverick. That's where the "Beautiful dog!" line came in.

There were several problems with the scene. The first was that no good rider would do what Skye was doing. It was very bad practice to canter a horse up to the stable. A horse was always supposed to be cooled down before being dismounted and stabled. Usually the last ten or fifteen minutes of any ride should be at a walk.

Lisa wanted to tell some of the people there about that, but nobody seemed to be interested in her horse expertise. Then it turned out that there was a worse problem, and it was Skye. According to the script, he was supposed to be excited and exhilarated by the ride. What he looked like was frightened.

Pepper had a wonderful rocking canter, but nobody would know that looking at Skye Ransom. He rode Pepper as if he were Ichabod Crane being chased by the headless horseman. There was a look of pure terror on his face.

"Cut!" Oliver cried out. "Something wrong, Skye?"

"No," Skye said, but it was clear that there was.

"Is the horse going too fast for you?" Oliver asked.

"No," Skye said. Lisa could tell that Skye was very uncomfortable about something, but she also knew that he was too much of a professional to let his problems cause trouble on the set. "Let's try it again, Oliver," he suggested.

Oliver agreed and the scene was set up again. Lisa returned to the stable, prepared to step out on cue. From the shadows, she watched Skye's approach. The second time wasn't any better than the first. The problem was that Skye was scared, pure and simple. When he drew Pepper to a halt and Oliver yelled "Cut," for the second time, Lisa tried to come to Skye's rescue. She stepped forward and took hold of Pepper's reins and began talking to the horse. She was really talking to Skye.

"Come on, boy, you can do this," she said. She patted Pepper on the neck and slipped a carrot stick in his mouth. "There's nothing to be afraid of. That's just a big old camera there, recording every beautiful, smooth move you make. Now, don't you go frightening my friend, Skye, okay? Just give him a smooth cantering gait that so he can rock like a baby in the saddle, okay, boy?"

"Okay, Lisa," Skye answered. He sounded a little testy. Lisa thought maybe she was being a little bit of a busybody. She backed off and waited while Skye and Oliver talked.

Maverick came over to her, wagging his tail eagerly. He was a welcome distraction to the discomfort around the set.

After the conference between Skye and Oliver, they tried the scene again. This time Skye managed to smile and look exhilarated all right, but it was because Red O'Malley, Pine Hollow's stable hand, made the mistake of driving a horse van right between Skye and the camera. Skye was laughing. When Red realized what he'd done, he jut drove off as quickly as he could. On the next take Maverick got distracted by one of the stable cats. And then it was Pepper's fault. He threw a shoe. The farrier happened to be at Pine Hollow and was able to put the shoe right back on. Pepper and Skye returned to their starting point for another try. This time Pepper had decided it was time to quit. As soon as Skye signaled him to canter, he began galloping so he could get back to Pine Hollow in a hurry. The look on Skye's face was anything but exhilaration.

"Cut!" Oliver cried, now very frustrated. "This isn't working, Skye," the director said, holding the horse's reins while Skye dismounted. "Is there something wrong with the horse?"

Skye shrugged and looked to Lisa for an answer.

"He could just be misbehaving," Lisa said. "I'll try riding him around for a minute to see if he calms down."

Lisa had learned that horses have moods just like people do, and sometimes when things start to go wrong, they get annoyed and misbehave. If that was what was wrong with Pepper, all she had to do was change his mood. She climbed into Pepper's saddle and began walking him. Right away she could tell he was in a bad mood because he was ambling slowly and reluctantly. It was almost as if he were trying to pick a fight. She signaled him to trot. He kept on walking. She tried again. He refused. No wonder Skye was having such a rough time with him! Pepper had been taking advantage of him from the start. It was hard to look exhilarated and happy when a horse was taking you for a ride instead of the other way around. Lisa tapped Pepper on the flank with a riding crop. He kept on walking. She did it again, a little harder, and he finally broke into a lumbering trot.

A riding crop wasn't meant to hurt a horse, and she certainly hadn't hurt Pepper. It was just supposed to remind him who was giving the orders. She tapped him again, and Pepper began to get the message. His trot perked up. For about five minutes Lisa rode Pepper around the paddock, changing gaits and directions. She wanted to fill his mind so full of her commands that he didn't have time to rebel. Pretty soon he was doing everything she told him, responding instantly to the slightest leg pressure or weight change. That was the way Pepper usually behaved.

"I think he's better now," Lisa said to Skye and Oliver. "He just needed to get a few kinks out." She dismounted and held the reins.

"Are you sure he's gotten *all* his kinks out?" Skye asked. "I wasn't having much fun, you know."

"Yes, we know," Oliver said stonily. "We have a couple of thousand dollars' worth of outtakes to prove it. And if we don't finish up today, we're going to have to hold over until tomorrow. We're supposed to be packed up and out of here by tonight, Skye. Are you ready to try again?"

Skye didn't like being reminded that these mistakes cost money. Lisa could see him wince at Oliver's testiness. He turned toward Pepper with a look of grim determination on his face.

"Hi-yo Silver," he said, trying to put on a bold face. He took the reins from Lisa, tightened up on them, and then grabbed hold of the saddle, putting his left foot in the stirrup. He shifted his weight onto his left foot and swung upward.

Pepper was as glad to have Skye returning to the saddle as Skye was to be there. The horse took several steps forward. Lisa grabbed for the bridle, barely getting hold of it and bringing Pepper to a stop before the horse took off with the star of the movie dangling by a leg. Skye's foot slid back out of the stirrup, his hands released their grip on the saddle, and he landed unceremoniously in the dirt. He glared at Pepper.

The tension was thick, and Lisa felt as if she were in the middle of it. After all, she was supposed to be Skye's riding coach, and she was the one who had said Pepper would behave. It seemed that Skye was about to start yelling at Pepper, and Oliver was about to start yelling at Skye. Lisa looked around desperately, hoping to find something like touching the good-luck horseshoe to break the mood.

Mother Nature suddenly came to the rescue. There was a tremendous gust of wind, bringing a chill to the air. Lisa looked up at the sky. Enormous gray clouds billowed overhead. The second gust of wind brought the first burst of rain.

The cameramen covered their equipment with tarps. Everybody else ran for cover.

Lisa brought Pepper into the stable. The horse looked out at the downpour uneasily. She realized, looking at him, that his moodiness may have been partly caused by the impending storm.

The whole crew stood watching the rain for about ten minutes until Oliver announced the obvious.

"This isn't going to stop soon," he said. "Let's change plans. We have an interior to shoot with some of the minor characters. You two," he said to Lisa and Skye. "Go get some schooltime in, and if it clears up, we'll try this scene again later. Otherwise, tomorrow."

Skye seemed very relieved. He turned and headed right for the makeshift classroom in Mrs. Reg's office. Lisa took Pepper back to his stall and untacked him. She didn't know if it was part of an actor's job to untack horses in movies, but she knew if she didn't take care of the horse, her "chaperone," Max, would give her a hard time.

It just took a few minutes, and when she arrived at the schoolroom, she found a history test in progress. The subject was Woodrow Wilson's Fourteen Points and the end of World War I. Lisa had studied that last semester and had reviewed it with Sabina this week. She took up paper and pencil and finished the test in a few minutes. Skye was done quickly, too. Alicia and Jesse took longer. The tutor excused Skye and Lisa. They withdrew to the tack room to talk. That way, Alicia and Jesse wouldn't be disturbed.

"Whew," Skye sighed, sitting down on a stepladder.

Lisa didn't know whether the sigh was relief about the history test or the rain that had stopped the day's filming. She looked at her watch. It was early afternoon. She was afraid that if the rain stopped, Oliver would want them to work late again. This was going to be her last chance to get to the mall with Stevie and Carole. She didn't mind working tomorrow morning, even though it was the day of the birthday party. She just didn't want to miss out on any more of the planning. She glanced out the window and was relieved to see the sky filled with dark and oppressive clouds.

"Good," she said, almost involuntarily.

"My feeling, exactly," Skye said. "I don't blame you for being angry with me."

"I'm not angry," Lisa said. "I'm just glad that it looks like it's going to keep on raining, because I want to leave on time today."

"What are you doing?" he asked.

Lisa told him about her conversations with Stevie and

Carole earlier in the week and how they were all going back to the mall to go shopping for the colonel—no matter what time she got out.

"It's just that the earlier, the better," she added.

"You really love doing that kind of thing, don't you?" Skye asked.

"Any kind of thing is more fun to do when I get to do it with Stevie and Carole."

Skye nodded knowingly. "I can see how that would be true." He sounded genuinely envious.

"Would you like to come along?" she asked. "Stevie and Carole would think that was a blast."

"It would be great," Skye said. "But remember our trip to the ice-cream place? It could be like that—only worse."

"Oh, yes," Lisa said, recalling the nightmare vividly. Lisa leaned back to consider the matter. If only there was a way to disguise Skye. Then a thought occurred to her. How hard could it be to create a disguise with all the facilities of a professional movie company at your disposal?

"What's that funny look on your face?" Skye asked.

"What look?" Lisa asked.

"It's sort of the way Stevie looks sometimes," Skye said.

Lisa giggled. "It must be because I'm getting an idea for

a Stevie-type scheme. See, if you hang around somebody long enough, you start to think the way they do. . . ."

"And?" he asked expectantly.

"And Stevie just came up with a wicked good idea to get you to the mall this afternoon." She grinned proudly. Then she stood up. "Let's get over to makeup and wardrobe."

"It's been tried before," Skye said, getting the idea. "And it usually doesn't work."

"It hasn't been tried the way The Saddle Club is going to do it!" Lisa told him.

TWO HOURS LATER the girls and Skye were ready. Oliver had called off filming Lisa and Skye's scene because of the rain, which was still pouring steadily. While Stevie and Carole made the final costume selection, Skye and Lisa enlisted Jeanette's aid.

With the help of a wig, Skye's straight sandy brown hair became unruly and blond. His eyes turned brown with contact lenses. A little bit of putty gave his nose a disjointed look, and some masterful strokes with pencils and brushes transformed his smooth, big-screen good looks into something that looked as if it had just stepped out of a dented pickup truck—and ought to be sent back to the farm as soon as possible!

"Do you want to be seen in public with me?" Skye asked, looking at the results of Jeanette's genius.

Lisa looked carefully at the none-too-appealing results. "Better in public than in private," she told him. "You definitely don't look like a movie star. People will be staying away instead of thronging after us. Can you stand it?"

"Hey, look at the T-shirt I found!" Stevie said, arriving breathlessly from the wardrobe trailer. Carole was close behind, carrying some ratty jeans and a pair of work boots to complete Skye's outfit. Stevie took the T-shirt and unfolded it. She held it up for everybody to admire. It read:

KORMAN'S EXTERMINATING
We get the bugs out!

"We're going to have the whole mall to ourselves!" Stevie said proudly as their newly invented friend, Gavin, slipped the T-shirt over his head carefully, so as not to disturb any of his makeup.

9

"WHERE TO FIRST?" Skye asked The Saddle Club as they
walked through the doors of the mall. It was a little difficult for him to talk with the wad of bubble gum he had in
his mouth—Stevie's final touch on his "disguise." Skye
blew an enormous bubble. A woman hurried past him as
if she were afraid she might catch something from him.

"Anywhere we want," Stevie said conspiratorially.

"Then it's pizza," Skye announced. "I haven't been
able to have a good oven-fresh pizza at a mall for a long
time."

"This way," Carole said. "It's at the far end of this aisle."

The foursome walked together, pausing to check out
some funny buttons and a collection of more moderate
T-shirts than the one "Gavin" was sporting.

"Hey, this one's cool," Stevie said, showing it to Skye. It was tie-dyed in long, sweeping arcs of rainbow colors.

To Stevie's surprise, Skye bought it.

"You never know when it might come in handy," he said, tucking the bag under his arm. They proceeded toward the pizza restaurant.

It took only a few minutes to come to an agreement on the toppings they wanted on their pizza.

"Extra cheese all over, ditto the pepperoni," Skye began, describing the pie they'd decided on. "Then, we want mushrooms on half and green peppers on half, but overlap the mushrooms fifty percent. Then, on the part that only has green peppers, add onions, okay? And sausage on the part that only has mushrooms. Got that?"

The waitress stared at him. Her eyes seemed to pierce right through him—and right through his disguise. The girls were sure she had recognized his voice and was about to reveal his identity. Stevie slid lower in her seat. Lisa tried to give Skye a menu to hide behind. Carole's eyes focused on a grease-stained map of Italy taped to the wall beyond their table. Skye, however, was fearless. He stared right back at the waitress.

The waitress drew in a deep breath. "You're going to take it the way we make it and you're going to *like* it," she said without blinking.

"Yes'm," Skye said, nodding meekly.

When the four of them were pretty sure the waitress was out of earshot, they exploded into laughter.

"Best performance in a supporting role!" Stevie announced when the laughter had died down.

"Aw, pshaw!" Skye said.

"Not you. Her!" Stevie told him. That made them all giggle some more.

When the pizza came, it was delicious, although nobody could tell, or remember, which slices were supposed to have which ingredients on them. The extra cheese covered everything and nobody cared.

They wanted to talk about the party as they ate, but they got sidetracked by talking about Colonel Hanson. The girls tried to describe him for Skye.

"He loves old movies," Carole said. "We sometimes stay up really later, munching popcorn, and watching the golden oldies. He likes anything about the Marine Corps, particularly if it stars John Wayne."

"*Sands of Iwo Jima!*" Skye blurted out.

"Number-one favorite," Carole confirmed.

"Me, too," said Skye.

"He also likes anything that has to do with the fifties and sixties," Lisa told Skye. "He can sing all the verses of everything Elvis Presley ever recorded. And the Everly Brothers, and even Bill Haley and the Comets."

"'Rock Around the Clock'!" Skye said. "I love it!"

"You're going to love him," Carole said. "I'm sure of it."

"Especially if you like the old jokes he tells," Stevie said. "He can go for hours with shaggy-dog stories, and elephant and grape jokes."

"What's big and purple and lives in the sea?" Skye asked Stevie.

"Moby Grape," she answered immediately. "Yes, indeed, you have passed the test. You're going to love Colonel Hanson."

"*If* we manage to put together a birthday party for him," Carole said ominously. "Now, where's your list, Lisa?"

Lisa stuck her hand into her pocket and produced her list. It was neatly written and organized.

"Okay," she began. "The first part of the list is the menu, and then there are the things we need to buy for that. That section is followed by everything we need to make this a real birthday party."

Stevie looked over her shoulder. "Crepe paper? Snappers? Hats? What is this—his fortieth or his fourth?"

"Who cares? It's a birthday party, isn't it?" Lisa said.

"What a great idea! What are you going to put in the goody bags?" Skye asked.

"My personal favorite is candy corn," Lisa said. "But I could be talked into bubble gum or licorice."

"We've got some serious shopping to do," Skye said. "Where to first?"

"This way," Stevie said, pointing to the checkout counter at the restaurant.

They each chipped in and paid their bill. Then they began their work in earnest.

They found a paper specialty store that had great party hats and balloons. They bought one of each for each guest. Then Skye suggested they get some noise-makers.

"Where will we go for that?" Lisa asked.

"I think I remember some in the party section of the variety store," Carole said, recalling her trip to the mall earlier in the week with Stevie. "It's over this way." She took them to the left.

There was nothing along that aisle but shoe stores.

"I think we're turned around," Stevie said. "We're headed right for Jeans' Korner. It's a great shop for girls' jeans, but not much for noisemakers."

They started to turn around when a couple of girls from the class ahead of Lisa's emerged from Jeans' Korner.

"Oh, it's Lisa!" the first one nearly shrieked. Her name was Patty, and she was prone to hysterical shrieks. She began running toward Lisa. "Is it true?" Patty asked breathlessly. "Are you really working with *Skye Ransom?*" She grabbed Lisa's arm dramatically.

Lisa flushed with embarrassment. She had no idea what to say.

Patty seemed to sense this was slightly embarrassing for Lisa. She looked at her friend's companions, and when she saw "Gavin," she began to realize what was going on. "Oh!" she shrieked.

Patty ran to get her friend. It was an escape opportunity The Saddle Club wasn't going to miss. Everyone looked to Stevie for help.

"This way!" Stevie hissed. She pulled her two friends and Skye into a perfume shop and dashed toward the rear of it. There was no time to ask questions. Everyone just followed Stevie.

"Head for bubble bath!" Stevie instructed. They dashed down an aisle, ducked to the right, and turned left, avoiding a clutch of teenage girls trying to decide on a cologne. The racing foursome moved so fast, the teenagers barely noticed them—they hoped.

Stevie took Skye's hand and led him and her friends behind a large display for a variety of fruit-flavored bubble baths.

"We'll be safe here," she assured them.

Carole wasn't so sure. She peered around the large

cardboard fruit tree, trying to look a little bit like a peach. She suspected she wasn't going to fool anybody. She withdrew into the shadows.

"Swell," she whispered. "Will we stay here until midnight, when the mall closes, or will we only have to wait until our parents send out the state police to search for us?"

"Neither," Stevie said. "We just have to change our cover."

Skye reached into his bag and pulled out the rainbow T-shirt. He slipped it on over Korman's Exterminating. Then he went into another bag and retrieved one of the silly hats they'd bought for the birthday paty. He put it on. It was hardly a make-over, but it might do the trick. With the makeup he was wearing, he didn't look much like Skye Ransom, and that was good, but he also didn't look like the boy the girls had come into the perfume shop with, either.

"Now, this way," Stevie said. She pasted an innocent smile on her face and stood up. Her friends joined her. It wasn't easy for Carole to look as if there were nothing unusual about hiding behind a seven-foot tall cardboard fruit tree, but she did her best. It turned out that nobody was looking.

Instead of going back up to the front of the store, Stevie went to the other rear corner. There was a door there.

"Where does it go?" Lisa asked.

"Out," Stevie answered simply. She opened it and they all went through it.

They found themselves in a long, dim corridor with a lot of nondescript doors along it.

"This must be some sort of back delivery entrance," Skye observed. It made sense. It also meant that they should be able to get into any number of stores from it— if only they could figure out where the doors led to.

They began opening them and peering through.

"Lingerie," Lisa announced.

"No way," Skye said. "Perfume was bad enough. Too many girls and women in those stores."

Carole opened the next door. "Movie rental—lots of men are in there. That's better, isn't it?"

"Only if they're not looking at boxes containing Skye's movies," Stevie said.

"Oh, right." Carole pulled the door closed.

Stevie opened the next door. "Nuts," she said.

"What's the matter?" Skye asked.

"It's a nut store," she explained.

"That sounds right for us," Carole said.

"Why? Because it's full of men?" Lisa asked.

"No, because I think we're nuts."

The logic was compelling. The four of them slipped through the door and into the little nut shop.

"I love cashews," Skye said.

"So does my dad," Carole said.

"Then let's get some for the party," Skye suggested. He asked for a pound. "See, shopping for a party isn't all that hard, is it?" he asked while the man weighed the nuts.

"It's not hard at all as long as you're willing to put on disguises and duck through back hallways in the mall," Lisa joked.

"It's him!" came the all-too-familiar shriek of Patty's voice.

"So much for that bright idea," Stevie said.

They quickly paid for the cashews, and then the four of them hightailed it right back through the delivery entrance of the nut shop and fled along the hall.

The whole thing might have been frightening if it hadn't been so funny. Lisa tried to run, but she became overwhelmed by the ludicrousness of the situation and began giggling helplessly.

Stevie noticed that Lisa had fallen behind and stopped to wait for her. Carole and Skye turned around. They saw Lisa leaning up against one of the plain gray walls, shaking uncontrollably.

"What's the matter with you?" Stevie asked. She sounded very concerned.

"It's just all so silly," Lisa said, lifting her head. Her friends saw then that she was laughing, not crying. "Here we are, with one of the most famous teenagers in the world, hiding behind cardboard trees, slipping in and out of ridiculous costumes, running through empty hallways away from screaming fans. I just keep thinking about the article this would make for *Teen Scene* magazine."

Even under all the makeup he was wearing, it was clear to see that Skye had paled.

"You wouldn't . . ." he uttered.

"No way!" Lisa assured him. "It's just that it's all so silly."

"I don't know how silly it is," Stevie said. "After all, those girls would tear the clothes off of him if they had a chance."

"Not my rainbow tie-dyed or my 'We get the bugs out!' T-shirts! I'll never let them have them!" Skye joked.

"And I bet this kind of thing happens to you all the time," Carole said.

Skye looked at her curiously. Then he looked down at himself, dressed to kill—cockroaches.

He started laughing just as hard as Lisa. He laughed

until the tears rolled down his cheeks, smearing his makeup.

"No," he said to Carole between giggles. "But I wish it did."

That was when Stevie and Carole joined in on the laughter. At that moment everything became funny: Skye's costume, their hiding place behind the tree, Patty's shriek, which became even funnier when Lisa described the time Patty had shrieked at a mouse that had gotten loose from the science lab in the school. Then they laughed at the idea that Skye, in his exterminator's outfit, should have been called in to help. They were totally exhausted from laughter by the time they finally found an exit to the parking lot of the shopping mall and tracked down Skye's limousine. Still giggling helplessly, they piled into the back of the car and giggled until they could giggle no more.

THE VIRGINIA COUNTRYSIDE whizzed by as Skye and The
Saddle Club rode back to Willow Creek in Skye's limousine. Skye opened the cooler and gave each of the girls
a soda. They were thirsty after all their adventures in the
back alleys of the shopping mall.

"You didn't tell us anything about your adventures in
front of the camera today," Stevie said to Lisa. "I mean,
was it easier? Did you do everything in one take today
like you've been doing all week?"

Lisa felt a sudden letdown. They'd had such fun at the
mall that she didn't like remembering that things really
hadn't gone well on the movie set today.

"Um, not exactly . . . ," Lisa began uncomfortably.

"Oh, I get it," Carole said. "You forgot your line.

Which was it today? The one about the dog, or just plain 'Awww'?"

"Um, well, a couple of things happened, and then there was the rain. We have to go back and shoot some things over tomorrow. It was no big deal, though."

She took a long drink of her soda, hoping she had managed to close the subject and hoping Stevie would shift to something else. No such luck, though.

"Lisa, you're trying not to tell me something," Stevie persisted. "What happened?"

"It was nothing," Lisa said. "Really."

Stevie was one of Lisa's best friends, and Lisa loved her an awful lot, but there were times when Stevie just couldn't take a hint. This was one of those times.

"I know! You tried to steal the scene and Skye's jealous!" Stevie teased.

"Stevie, please!" Lisa said, now almost irritated.

Carole tugged at Stevie's sleeve. That didn't work, either. Stevie was about to come up with something else when Skye spoke up.

"It was a terrible day on the set, Stevie," he said. "And it wasn't just because of the rain. Lisa is trying to be nice. She did everything right. I did everything wrong. We were filming an easy scene and I couldn't get it. I had trouble with Pepper, but that wasn't all. I had trouble with everything. Oliver is furious with me. We have to

STAR RIDER

hold over the filming until tomorrow, and I'm going to hear an awful lot about how much that is going to cost. Even worse, I'm not at all sure I'm going to do the scene any better tomorrow than I did today. I was not meant to be a horseback rider. Period."

Suddenly Stevie was all seriousness. She could tease Lisa, but she'd never tease Skye. "Everybody has days like that," she said, trying to reassure him.

"Not me," he insisted. "I wanted to blame the horse, but it wasn't really his fault. I was the one who couldn't control him. I was the one who couldn't perform, either as a rider or as an actor. I know Oliver was upset."

"Oh, come on, Skye," Lisa said. "You're being hard on yourself. You just had a bad day. Tomorrow will be another day and it will be better."

"When tomorrow comes, I'll have to get back on Pepper and I'll have to pretend I'm not frightened. That's going to call for more acting skill than I have."

Lisa felt bad for Skye. She and her friends loved horses and weren't afraid of them. She hated to think how much fun she would miss if she were afraid of them and didn't ride. But in Skye's case, being afraid wasn't just cutting him out of a lot of fun on horseback, it was interfering with what he did best—and that was acting.

Stevie had another idea, though. "Sure you've got acting skills that you can rely on, Skye, but you've got something even more important than that. You've got The Saddle Club to rely on."

"Hear, hear," Carole added. Skye smiled. "And now that we've taken care of that problem, let's get on to the bigger one—Dad's birthday party. After all, it *is* tomorrow night."

"We've got hats and nuts," Lisa said, trying to be optimistic. "What else do we need?"

"If you want my opinion, the best birthday parties are the classics," Skye said. "I mean, when I think 'birthday party,' I think of games like treasure hunts and Pin the Tail on the Donkey."

"Oh, come on," Lisa said.

"No, really. Or else how about the kind of party where they have a magician?"

"Dad loves magic shows," Carole said. "A magician would be just about perfect. And, to tell you the truth, I kind of like the idea of a sort of child's birthday party for the child in my father."

"Not a bad idea," Stevie confirmed. "Sometimes it seems that the child in your father is about eighty-five percent of him!"

"Stevie!" Lisa said. "That's not nice!"

"Yes, it is," Carole said. "And it's true. It's one of the things that makes Dad so wonderful. The other fifteen percent—the grown-up part—is lovable, too."

"And how about the half of him that sometimes drives you crazy?" Stevie asked.

Carole and Lisa exchanged looks. "No wonder she comes to us for help with her math homework," Carole said. Stevie had the good grace to smile.

The glass window separating the girls and Skye from the driver lowered slowly.

"We're coming into Willow Creek, Mr. Ransom. Where to first?" the driver asked politely.

"Once more around the park, James," Skye said. "We've got some planning to do."

"Very good, sir," the driver said. He winked at the four conspirators and made the window rise noiselessly.

"I think I'm beginning to get the idea of how this is going to work," Skye said. "Lisa, let's make a list."

Lisa reached into her pocketbook and pulled out her notebook and pencil.

"Now, here's how it goes," Skye began authoritatively. "First thing to put on the list is 'one magician.'"

Lisa wrote it dutifully, but Carole was more than a little concerned.

"Where are we going to get a magician?" she asked. "And how are we going to pay for it? I mean our budget barely allows for a pound of cashews, much less a full-fledged magician. Maybe, if I could get Dad to let me take some money out of my college account, or even out of the money that I'm using to pay for Starlight's boarding. . . . What *are* you doing?" she asked Skye when she realized that he wasn't paying any attention at all to her talk about funding the magician.

Skye was wiggling his fingers nimbly in the air, almost as if he were trying to do some warm-up exercises with them.

"Yeah, what are you doing?" Stevie asked.

"Oh, not much," Skye said. "I was just going to see what that is that you have stuck behind your ear."

Then, before Stevie even had time to react, Skye reached for her head, brushed back her long hair, and pulled his hand back, revealing a quarter.

"And somebody once accused me of being a gold digger," Skye said. "I'm really much more interested in silver. But sometimes . . ." He reached for the edge of Carole's sleeve. "I like copper." He handed her the penny he had "pulled" out of her sleeve.

Lisa's eyes opened wide with wonder. "How did you do that?"

"A magician never reveals his secrets," Skye said mysteriously. "He does, however, rise to any occasion on which his magic arts are required. Did you say something about wanting a magician for your father's birthday party?"

"You would?" Carole said, jumping ahead.

"Why not?" Skye said. "After all, it's something I can do—unlike riding a horse. And since we have to film tomorrow, I'll just happen to be around. Do I get an invitation?"

"Oh, Skye!" Carole said excitedly. "Dad is just going to love it!"

She flung her arms around the surprised boy and gave him a big hug. He hugged her back.

IT WAS HARD for Lisa to believe that this was actually going to be her last day of filming. The whole experience had been a little surreal—like a dream that was almost too real—but now it was nearly over. Lisa found she was getting used to the crazy schedule of classes one minute, rehearsals the next, tests, and filming. She was no longer confused by the arrival and departure of students in the class, or upset by retakes, close-ups, and cameras that sometimes traveled on railroad tracks to follow a moving performer. It had somehow all become routine.

"Lisa, who was the French representative to the peace talks after World War I?" the tutor asked.

"Georges Clemenceau," she answered promptly.

"Is this her last day?" Alicia asked. "I hope so, because

she's showing up the rest of us." Lisa had the feeling she was only half joking.

"Lisa applies herself to her studies," the tutor said. "You might learn from her."

The classroom door opened abruptly. John stuck his head in. "Lisa, Skye, you're wanted on the set. It's time for the reshoot of scene twenty-three."

Lisa and Skye stood up to leave. Lisa couldn't help noticing a look of great discomfort on Skye's face. Scene twenty-three was the one where he had to canter up to the stable.

"You'll be fine," Lisa said, not thinking that anybody else would overhear her. She was wrong, though. Alicia overheard her, and she didn't miss the opportunity to make the best of it.

"That's right, Skye. All you have to do is apply yourself," Alicia said, mimicking the tutor. There were a couple of snickers.

"Thanks," Skye said good-naturedly, and then smiled. His grin, which had won the hearts of millions of moviegoers, took the sting out of Alicia's teasing. "C'mon, let's go," he said to Lisa. "Let's go break a leg."

"Pepper's leg?" Lisa joked.

Then all the kids in the class laughed. It was clear to

everybody that what was wrong with scene twenty-three was between Skye and Pepper.

MAVERICK GREETED BOTH Lisa and Skye warmly when they arrived at the paddock where the scene was to be shot. Lisa knelt down and gave the dog a big hug.

"Good, Lisa, that's just what we want," Oliver said. "Now let's hear your line."

Lisa looked up, imagining she was seeing Skye on horseback.

"Beautiful dog!" she said. She was supposed to sound sincere. It wasn't hard. Maverick *was* a beautiful dog. He was also licking her ear and it tickled. She laughed.

"Nice job," Oliver said, "except cut out the giggle, okay?"

"Yes, sir," Lisa said obediently. That meant she was done with her part of the rehearsal. John showed her where to wait in the stable while Skye readied himself for the scene. One of the production assistants walked out of the stable with Pepper. Lisa gave him a reassuring pat. It was her way of telling Pepper to be good to Skye. She thought she ought to give Skye a reassuring pat, too, so he'd be good to Pepper!

She held Pepper's bridle while Skye mounted him. While she did that, she rubbed Pepper's cheek. It was a pat that horses just loved. She thought maybe he smiled at her. That was a good sign. She just wished Skye could smile, too. He looked very uncomfortable. She wanted to help him in any way she could. She wished she could be with him in the woods when he began the canter toward the stable. That would help. Still, there was something . . .

"Okay, Skye, let's begin," Oliver said.

"Wait a sec, Skye," Lisa interrupted, suddenly remembering something. "You forgot the good-luck horseshoe."

Skye looked at her doubtfully. "I think this is going to take more than a horseshoe." Still, he reached over and brushed the worn iron shoe that was nailed to the stable door. Then a stable hand took the horse's bridle and led Skye outside. Since Lisa's instructions were to wait inside until they were ready for her in about ten minutes, she couldn't see what was going on. Considering the last look she'd seen on Skye's face, maybe that was for the better.

Lisa didn't mind waiting in the stable. She was always happy in the Pine Hollow stables. She saw that Veronica diAngelo's horse, Garnet, needed some fresh water. She took the mare's bucket and filled it at the tap. Garnet drank deeply and seemed to thank Lisa with her eyes. Garnet didn't get much attention from Veronica. Lisa wished she owned a horse like Garnet—*her* horse would get all the attention it could possibly want.

Patch, a pinto gelding, was the first horse Lisa had ever ridden at Pine Hollow. Although she didn't ride him much now, she always felt a special warmth toward him. He needed some hay. She took a flake of hay from a nearby bale and put it into his feeder. He munched contentedly.

Lisa walked along the aisle until she came to Starlight's stall. As long as she was checking on special horses, she certainly ought to include Carole's own Starlight. But Lisa didn't see him there. She walked right up to the door of the stall and stood on tiptoe to see if he'd decided to lie down and rest, but there was no sign of him.

That was odd. Very few people except Carole would ever ride him, and she hadn't seen Carole that morning. Would Carole come into the stable and take Starlight out without even saying hello to her? Besides, Carole was supposed to be at home, setting up the birthday party for tonight.

Confused, Lisa decided to investigate further. She walked around to the other side of the aisle to Topside's stall. He was missing, too. Next, she checked the tack room. As she was beginning to suspect, Starlight's and Topside's tacks were both missing. The only thing it could mean was that Stevie and Carole had gone riding without her.

Lisa felt an odd twinge. As much as she was enjoying being part of the movie and working with Skye Ransom—the dream of only about one hundred million girls around the world—she once again felt that she was missing something, and that something was her friends. There she was, standing in a stable, surrounded by horses she couldn't ride, waiting to be told when she should come outside and say "Beautiful dog!" while her friends were having a wonderful ride in the fields and woods around Pine Hollow.

Then she reminded herself that the movie-making would be over soon enough. Tonight there was Colonel Hanson's birthday party, and tomorrow she could go for a ride with Stevie and Carole. She had a lot to look forward to while she waited for her cue.

People often told Skye Ransom that he was a perfectionist. He always thought it was a compliment, although some people didn't say it in a way that sounded like a compliment. What they meant, he suspected, was that he always tried too hard, made too much of too many little problems. Good enough should be good enough. But good enough wasn't enough for Skye. Best was what he insisted upon, always.

Oliver believed that it was important for an actor to understand the motivation of the character he was playing. The director had been over Gavin's character and motivation so many times, Skye thought he could recite the speech himself.

"He's a boy who loves animals. He can practically understand what's on their minds. It's people Gavin doesn't understand."

That was where Skye and Gavin split. Skye loved people—as long as they weren't chasing him. He liked a lot of animals, including Maverick, but he didn't understand horses at all. Horses were big. They could move fast, and they seemed to have a knack of trying to get him out of the saddles on their backs. He'd fallen off of horses' backs more often than he wanted to recall. He didn't want to do it again in front of a camera.

Pepper sensed Skye's nervousness and took advantage of it right away. Skye could feel the horse taking charge. He was afraid that this day's shooting was going to be a carbon copy of their last attempt at this scene. That wouldn't be good enough by anyone's standards.

"Okay, take your place, Skye," Oliver said. "Let's do this and do it right, okay?"

Skye nodded. He turned Pepper around and headed for the wooded area where he was to begin riding. He knew what to do. He'd done it often enough; he'd just done it wrong before. He wanted, more than anything, to do it right this time.

Pepper trotted willingly into the woods. Skye liked riding in woody areas. He enjoyed the fresh green of the trees and the quiet of the forest. He hoped it would give him a chance to collect his thoughts and become Gavin, the boy who wasn't afraid of animals.

"Hi, there, pardner!" a familiar voice greeted him.

It was Stevie and she was on horseback. There, next to her, was Carole, riding Starlight.

"Hi! What are you two doing here? Does Oliver know?"

"Of course not," Stevie whispered. "Nobody's allowed to be anywhere near the set, but we have our ways, and we figured out how to get here without anybody noticing. You don't mind, do you?"

"I don't think so, although I'm not too crazy about the idea of a couple of people I like a lot watching me blow this scene one more time."

"That's what we're here for," Carole said.

"To watch me blow it?" Skye asked, a little horrified.

"No, that's not what she means," Stevie said. "We're here to keep you from blowing it. Remember? I told you that you had The Saddle Club behind you. We won't let you down."

"The Saddle Club is a real full-service organization, isn't it?"

"We aim to please," Carole said, and she meant it. She

and Stevie had decided the day before that they just had to keep Skye from messing up again. For one thing, they liked him and they wanted to help him. For another, he seemed so upset about having failed that they didn't want him to have to go through that again.

"Now, first things first," Carole continued. She hoped she sounded a little bit like a Marine Corps colonel. She wanted Skye to know that she knew what she was talking about. "When you're riding at a canter, you have to do two things that seem impossible to do at once. You have to sit up straight and you have to rock with the motion of the horse, shifting your weight as he shifts his from front to back."

"Aw, come on—" he began to protest.

"And here's how you do it," Carole went on authoritatively. "Your lower body has to be relaxed, almost as if it were draped around the saddle. Your knees have to be relaxed enough to flex with the forward motion of your body. That happens automatically, though, as long as you're not gripping for your life with your knees. The part of your body that you have to consciously allow to move is your hips. That's where the rocking in the saddle part starts. The upper part of your body doesn't have to be rigid, but it helps if you pretend that you are a puppet suspended from a string that comes from the button in your hat. It holds you nice and tall in the saddle."

"That's a lot to learn in the next five minutes," Skye said, complaining.

"It isn't," Carole insisted. "It's not hard because it's right. If you're doing it right, it feels right and you know it."

Skye looked as if he were going to protest. Stevie decided not to give him the chance.

"Try it," she said. "Let's take a little ride together away from the camera." She shifted her weight and Topside began walking. She reached back with her left foot and touched him behind his girth. Topside immediately began his rhythmic canter. Pepper followed suit. Carole, on Starlight, came up at the end.

"Let your legs hang," she said. "They are very heavy." Skye's legs relaxed immediately. As a result, Pepper's stride relaxed and became smoother.

"Sit up! The string is pulling you straight up!" Carole said.

Skye rose in the saddle, still allowing his hips to move with Pepper's strides.

"Much better!" Carole said, very pleased with her lesson.

Stevie circled around in a clearing in the woods and led the way back to Skye's starting point. She pulled gently on Topside's reins, and she and her friends all came to a stop.

"You did it!" Skye said.

"No, *you* did it," Carole insisted.

"Well, whoever was responsible, it worked. Thank you. Now all you have to do is remind me of everything right before I go—and it looks like they are about ready for me," he said, glancing through the woods. "What is it again?"

"Don't worry, you'll know," Carole said. "It's like riding a bicycle."

"Besides," added Stevie, "if we run over the rules again, that's all that will be on your mind. You can't look exhilarated if you're thinking about strings out of the top of your head and hips sliding in the saddle!"

Skye laughed.

"*Places!*" a megaphone shrieked from the stable.

Skye's laughter stopped. His face became stony, and he looked as if he were concentrating very hard on something.

"Uh-oh," said Carole. "That expression is definitely *not* exhilarated."

"Skye, did you hear the one about the three vampires who went into a bar?" Stevie asked.

"Huh?" Skye said.

"Three vampires," Stevie repeated. "They went into a bar and sat down at a table. The waitress came over to take their order."

"Stevie!" Skye said. He was trying hard to concentrate, but that was the last thing Stevie and Carole thought he ought to be doing. Stevie persisted.

"The first one said, 'I'll have a blood.' The waitress wrote that down. She looked at the second one. 'Same for me,' he said."

"*Lights! Camera!*" the megaphone blurted. Stevie had to hurry.

"The waitress looked at the third vampire. 'I'll just have some plasma,' he said. The waitress jotted that down, too. She turned to the bartender and said, 'Two bloods and a blood light!'"

Skye started laughing.

"Two bloods and a blood light!" He repeated the punch line between bursts of laughter. "That's a good one!"

"*Action!*"

Without thinking, Skye signaled Pepper to begin their scene. The horse responded instantly. The last thing Stevie and Carole saw as Skye rode away was that he was still grinning at the silly joke. He was so focused on the joke that he wasn't even noticing that his legs hung like heavy weights around the horse's belly, his hips swayed easily with Pepper's gait, and his torso sat straight up, as if suspended from the sky.

"He looks exhilarated, don't you think?" Stevie asked Carole.

"Definitely," she agreed.

"NOW!" A PRODUCTION assistant signaled Lisa. She stepped out of the shadow of the stable and watched Skye approach. Maverick bounded out from the underbrush and kept pace with Pepper's gait. The most astonishing thing, however, was the look of exhilaration on Skye's face. Lisa grinned just looking at him.

Maverick arrived first. Lisa knelt down and gave him a pat and a hug. He licked her face. She nuzzled against his soft fur.

"Beautiful dog!" Lisa said to Skye. Saying that line wasn't acting at all.

"Thanks," he said. "Here, take my horse, will you? Give him some extra grain today. He really deserves it!" Skye looked as if saying that line wasn't acting, either. Lisa wondered what had happened to make it all work so well, but whatever it was, she was grateful for it.

She took Pepper's reins and led him into the stable.

"That's a take! Print it! Great job, Skye!" Oliver said. There was a lot of relief in his voice.

"Thanks," Skye said.

"What's your secret?" Oliver asked.

"Oh, I don't know. I guess it's that, like Gavin, I've learned you can do anything with a little help from your friends."

He winked at Lisa. She didn't have any idea why he did that, but then she remembered the two horses missing from their stalls. Whatever Stevie and Carole were up to, it worked. She winked back.

"That's a wrap, Lisa," Oliver said. "You're all done here and you can go on home. It's been a pleasure having you work with us. I think we've all learned something from you." He shook her hand and then turned to his cameramen. "Now, for the close-ups . . ."

It was over. She was being dismissed. Lisa's moment as a star was done. She wanted to talk to Skye, but he was immediately drawn into a rehearsal for the next scene. He had only a second to wave good-bye. "I'll see you at Carole's at six, I hope," he said, and then he was gone.

Lisa wanted to talk to Stevie and Carole, but they were nowhere to be seen.

Now that the end of her career as a film actress had come, she wanted to share her thoughts with someone, almost anyone. She looked up. She realized she was still holding Pepper's reins. "Come on," she said. "I'll tell *you* all about it."

Slowly she led the horse back into the stable, where she untacked and groomed him.

A few minutes later, Stevie and Carole arrived.

"We've got loads of stuff to do!" Carole said, untacking

Starlight quickly. "We've got to set up the table and pick up the cake, and then we have to—"

"Talk," Lisa said, interrupting. "We have to *talk*."

"Of course, that, too," Stevie said. "There's lots to talk about and lots to tell."

"Horses come first," Carole said. That was just like Carole to insist that they take care of the horses before satisfying their own curiosities. They were so curious that taking care of the horses took only a few minutes.

The three of them linked arms and headed for the door of the stable. They almost couldn't get through, though, because of the overnight express delivery man, trundling up the path to the stable, carrying three giant cardboard cartons.

"Somebody here named Ransom?" he asked.

"That way," Stevie said, pointing through the stable. "You'll find him wherever somebody is yelling 'Action!'"

The delivery man gave her a weird look, but followed her directions through the stable.

"Now, speaking of 'somebody here named Ransom,' what were you two up to in the woods with Skye?" Lisa asked. "Don't try to fool me; I know you were there."

Carole and Stevie exchanged looks. "Did you hear the one about the three vampires?" Stevie asked.

IT WAS TIME. At six-thirty Carole and her friends and her father's friends ducked behind all the furniture in the Hansons' living room. Two people stood behind the drapes. Several more ducked into the dining room and were prepared to pop open the double doors at just the right moment. The house was silent.

Colonel Hanson marched up the walk. The thing about being a Marine was that he always marched everywhere. Carole could tell her father's march from a great distance. Now it wasn't a distance away, it was just a few feet from the door. He climbed up the steps onto the porch.

Thump. Thump. Thump.

There was silence for a few seconds. Carole knew her father was reaching in his pocket for his keys. She heard the familiar jingle of his key ring. She held her breath. The key scritched as he slid it into the lock. He turned the key, the lock released.

Thump. Thump. Thump. He was inside. The door closed behind him.

"Carole? You home?"

"*Surprise!*" The word burst out in chorus from all the guests. The dining-room doors flew open. More guests popped out. The drapes flapped aside. "Surprise!"

Colonel Hanson was bowled over with astonishment. His jaw dropped, his eyes opened wide.

"For me?" he asked, looking around at the crepe paper that festooned the living room.

"Of course it's for you!" Stevie said. "Is it anybody else's birthday? Did you really think we were going to ignore your birthday when you're turning so *old*?"

Colonel Hanson turned to his daughter. "Who was in charge of the guest list? Do I get to uninvite people who make fun of my age?"

"Sure," Carole said. "Unless it's Stevie. She's practically the mastermind of this whole operation. She's got to stay."

"Oh, all right," he said, pretending to be annoyed, but he gave Stevie a hug, which he knew she deserved.

"Anyway, you look like you could use a party," Lisa

said. She took him by the hand and led him to the dining room, where she poured him a glass of punch.

Lisa was thrilled with the fact that they'd surprised the colonel, and she knew it was going to be a fun party, but there was one thing missing. Skye hadn't shown up. Movie-making was unpredictable, she had certainly learned, but she had hoped Skye would be able to leave the set in time to join in on the fun. After all, it was just his kind of party.

By then all of the guests were helping themselves to the goodies that the girls had laid out. In keeping with the theme of a children's party, there wasn't a vitamin in sight. There were brownies and Rice Krispies treats. There were even peanut butter and jelly sandwiches. Stevie had wanted to figure out a way to make s'mores—her personal favorite junk food—but Carole wouldn't let her light a fire in the barbecue. It didn't matter, though; everybody seemed to be having a great time.

Colonel Hanson was thrilled with everything The Saddle Club had done for his birthday party. He loved the punch and the food; he loved the hats and the noise-makers. It turned out that they weren't just noisemakers. They were slide whistles that could make different notes. Colonel Hanson got all his guests to play "Row, Row, Row Your Boat" and then divided them into groups so they could do it as a round. A lot of people had trouble with that, because it's hard to laugh and play a slide whistle at the same time.

"This is the sloppiest group of musicians I've ever seen. Next year, kazoos!" called Colonel Hanson.

"Do we have to give you a big party again like this next year?" Stevie asked. "I mean, forty-one isn't exactly a milestone like forty."

"Who says I'm going to be forty-one next year?" the colonel asked. "I think of this as my *first* fortieth birthday!"

"No way!" Carole said. "Do you know how much time we spent at the mall to put this thing together?"

The grown-ups looked at the girls and in a single voice said "Awwww," very unsympathetically. Carole had to agree; spending time at the mall wasn't exactly punishment.

"Okay, okay," she relented. "But anyway, the party isn't over yet. You have some presents to open."

With that, all the guests returned to the living room and the colonel began opening his gifts. Colonel Hanson wasn't hard to buy presents for. If it was funny, or if it was from the fifties or sixties, he wanted it.

One of his friends gave him a whole book of elephant jokes.

"Oh, no," groaned two of the people who worked in

his office. "Do you know what this means?" one of them asked.

The other nodded. "Weeks of dreadful jokes. We try to limit him to one a day, but you know how he is."

Carole's father started flipping through the book, looking for just the right joke for this occasion.

"I think you'd better open another present, Dad, before everybody leaves!"

The next present was a matchbox car—an Edsel, which was a very famous failure in the late fifties. Colonel Hanson loved it.

There were Hawaiian shirts, Groucho Marx glasses, a videotape of a Jerry Lewis movie, a broken guitar string that the giver swore had probably belonged to Elvis Presley, and a tube of Brylcreem—hair oil of the fifties.

Lisa watched, enjoying Colonel Hanson's pleasure with each gift. They were fun and silly, and the whole room seemed to be filled with love and happiness. Still, she couldn't help feeling disappointed that Skye hadn't shown up yet. She looked at her watch. She glanced out the window. She laughed at all the jokes, but there was a little bit of emptiness inside. Where was Skye?

"It's time for games!" Stevie announced. They had set up Pin the Tail on the Donkey in the dining room. Colonel Hanson's aide won, hands down, although a few of the guests suggested he was cheating by peeking out the bottom of the blindfold.

"How else would I know where the firing squad was?" the aide asked, defending himself. Everybody laughed.

Next was musical chairs, with music from the fifties, of course. Carole had chosen the soundtrack of Elvis Presley's film *G.I. Blues*, because it seemed to fit with all the military people at the party. Stevie won the game, although she'd had to steal the last chair from a major.

"I think I left my flank uncovered," the major said, leaving the game sheepishly.

Lisa didn't feel like playing games and tried to stay on the sidelines, but Stevie insisted that she join in on dunking for apples. She wasn't very good at it, and she knew it. In fact, she had to hold her breath and stick her whole face into the water just to get her teeth into the apple. She emerged with her eyes shut tight, water dripping from her face and hair, but triumphant, an apple dangling precariously from her teeth—to hear none other than Skye Ransom say, "You never looked more beautiful!"

Her jaw dropped, and the apple splashed back into the bucket.

"You lose!" Stevie declared, but Lisa thought she was wrong. Now that Skye was there, she couldn't lose!

13

ONCE LISA GOT the water out of her eyes and dried her face and hair, she realized that Skye was not alone. He was accompanied by the chauffeur, who was totally laden with some large overnight express delivery boxes that definitely looked familiar.

"I had magic tricks sent from home," Skye explained. "I mean, you can't have a magic show without tricks, can you?"

"The whole thing?" she said, quite stunned.

"Not everything. I just couldn't ask my father to pack up the box I use to saw a lady in half. Besides, I like you the way you are!"

"Aww," Lisa said, perfectly imitating her line from the movie.

"Stop trying to impress me with your acting ability," he teased. "Give me a hand."

Skye and Lisa shooed everybody out of the family room and closed the doors to set up the show.

"I wonder what's going on in there," Stevie said to Carole.

"Magic," Carole told her. "Pure magic."

Stevie thought that was probably true.

After a while Lisa came out and told Stevie to invite all the guests in for the performance. There was a buzz of excitement. Everyone was curious about Skye Ransom's magic show.

Colonel Hanson was given the seat of honor—his own lounge chair. The other guests found seats, perched on tables, or just plain sat on the floor.

"Ladeez and Gentlemen!" Stevie began, sounding very much like a circus barker. "Saddle Club Entertainment Group is proud to present our very own Lisa Atwood and her assistant, uh, Cloud, uh, Storm, uh, whatzisname? Oh, yeah, Skye—"

"Quit the introduction. Let's get on with the show!" Carole insisted.

"Sure," Stevie said agreeably. "Anyway, you know who they are. Now let's see how good they are!"

Lisa and Skye stood up and the guests applauded. Lisa had no idea what she was doing, but it didn't matter, because Skye knew exactly what he was doing. He had the benefit of some very good and very expensive tricks, but a magician is only as good a magician as he is a performer. Skye was a terrific performer.

He bowed graciously and began his tricks right away. First, he found some coins behind some of the guests' ears—quarters, fifty-cent pieces. He even found a silver dollar behind the colonel's ear. One of the guests was the colonel's boss—a general. Naturally, what Skye pulled out from behind *his* ear was a piece of brass!

Skye believed in keeping things moving too quickly for the guests even to have time to wonder how he'd done them. Lisa was astonished at his speed. He moved from appearing and disappearing coins, to card tricks. Then, pretty soon, he was pouring milk into one glass and drinking it out of another. Glasses, bottles, oranges, even the colonel's hat appeared, disappeared, and moved around, seemingly at will—definitely at Skye's will! Lisa couldn't keep up with it all, and she loved every minute of it.

She found herself holding a teeny little box, out of which emerged twenty yards of silk scarves. She knew they couldn't possibly be coming out of the tiny box in her hand, but she didn't know where they did come from. Skye was so skillful, even his assistant was left in the dark. She was even more in the dark when he put all the scarves back in the box. For a minute she considered trying to figure out how he'd done it, then she decided it didn't matter. It was entertainment, and it was terrific.

For a grand finale Skye removed the silk top hat he'd worn throughout the show.

"This thing hasn't been fitting me right," he said a little irritatedly. "I bought it from the best hatter in Beverly Hills—a funny little guy named Katz. He told me it might be a little uncomfortable the first few times I wore it. He said a hat takes time to adjust from the hatter to the wearer. So I guess what I'm doing is working the Katz out of this one." Skye ran his hands around the outside of the hat. "Nice and smooth here," he said. Then he looked into the hat. "Hmmm," he said, "I think I see what the problem might be." He reached into the hat. There was an odd sound. "Here we go!" Skye said triumphantly. "I think I've figured out how to work the Katz out." He brought his hand out of the hat, and in it he was holding Carole's cat, Snowball! He handed the astonished cat to an even more astonished Carole and put the hat back on his head. "Fits perfectly now!" He bowed to the loud clapping and cheers of all the guests crowded into Carole's family room.

The colonel shook his hand and the girls all hugged him.

"You were wonderful!" Carole said.

"You just *made* the party," Lisa agreed heartily.

"How *did* you do it?" Stevie asked.

"Magicians never tell," Skye said mysteriously. "Now let's clear the decks a little bit, because I have some more entertainment, and this is the place for it." He took out a large tablecloth and spread it over the table of tricks. Then he took one box, which had been set aside, and opened it. Inside was a videotape cassette.

"I think you're going to like this, too," he said to everybody, slipping the tape into the Hansons' VCR. "It's sort of a magic show—in its own way." Curious, Carole pushed some buttons, and the tape began.

It took a few seconds for the girls to recognize what it was, but it was Lisa who knew first.

"It's the scene we filmed this morning!" she said. "Look, here comes Skye!"

Indeed, there he came. First there was the sound of hoofbeats, then Pepper came cantering out of the woods with Skye in the saddle. There was a big exhilarated grin on his face. Maverick came loping around the other side of a bush and ran alongside Pepper, arriving at the stable first. The camera drew back. There was Lisa. Maverick ran up to her. She hunkered down to greet the dog, who licked her face eagerly.

"Beautiful dog!" she said to Skye as he pulled Pepper to a halt in front of her.

Lisa was entranced. All of the surreal feelings she'd had during the filming came back to her. She couldn't believe she was actually looking at herself. She scrunched her eyes closed, almost trying to clear her vision, but it was still Lisa on the screen when she opened them again. It was real.

"Now look at this," Skye said. Lisa didn't know what to expect. The scene was over. Skye had dismounted and she'd taken Pepper's reins. She heard Oliver yell "Cut," but the camera kept on rolling. It panned slowly back over the route Skye had taken out of the woods. It stopped, capturing two riders on horseback, watching the events of the filming by the stable.

"It's us!" Stevie shrieked with pleasure, and she was right. There were Stevie and Carole on horseback, watching every move Skye and Lisa made and completely unaware of the camera that watched them. Then the screen went blank.

"You were wonderful," Skye said. "I couldn't have done it without you—all three of you. As a matter of fact, I didn't think I was going to be able to do it at all. I asked my uncle to make a videotape so I could study it to see what I was doing wrong. Instead I learned what my friends were doing right." He smiled at The Saddle Club. "Thank you *very* much."

Colonel Hanson stood up from his lounge chair and

reached out to shake Skye's hand. "This has been great, Skye. You've given me a couple of wonderful birthday presents."

"But I'm not quite done, sir," Skye said.

"There's more?"

"Yes, and from what I know of you, you might like this the best. You see, there were these three vampires who went into a bar . . ."

"COME ON, LET'S go this way," Stevie said, looking back over her shoulder at the two riders behind her. The three of them had decided to have a mounted Saddle Club meeting. That way they could talk about the colonel's wonderful birthday, and all of the excitement of the week that had just passed, during the privacy of their own ride.

It was early Sunday morning. The sun had been up just over an hour and the morning was cool. The movie company had packed up and left Pine Hollow the previous evening, departing almost as quickly as they'd come. Pine Hollow wasn't a movie set anymore, it was back to being a wonderful place to ride horses. Being a movie set had been exciting. Being a place to ride horses was better. The girls had found themselves relieved to see that the trucks and vans were all gone.

The horses sensed the excitement of their riders and trotted briskly through the field behind Pine Hollow. They were headed for a big rock by the creek that had given the town of Willow Creek its name. It was a favorite spot for The Saddle Club.

Lisa loved riding Pepper, and she thought he deserved the pleasure of a nice early-morning ride to reward him for all of his hard work in a starring role in a movie. She leaned forward and patted him appreciatively on the neck.

"There she goes, trying to make friends with another star," Carole teased.

"I'm just thanking him for taking care of Skye," she said. Carole understood.

In a few minutes they were in the shade of the forest and following the trail to the creek. The horses seemed to know the way by themselves.

They drew to a halt at the edge of the water. The girls dismounted and secured the horses to a tree branch with lead ropes they'd each brought along.

"Can you believe it's all over?" Stevie asked. She sat down on the rock and leaned back against the trunk of a tree.

"What a week!" Lisa agreed. "Did it really happen?"

"Want me to pinch you?" Stevie offered.

"No thanks," Lisa told her.

"It was a wonderful week," Carole agreed. "So many exciting things were going on. The movie, Skye, the party . . . I kind of hate to have it end."

"Not me," Lisa said. "It was fun, but I, for one, am ready for normal again. I mean, Skye is a nice guy and he lives this wonderful life, where he has a limousine wherever he wants one and somebody will ship a whole magic show for him at the drop of a silk top hat, but I wouldn't change lives with him for anything."

"Because of all the screaming girls that follow him all the time?" Stevie asked.

"No, because he doesn't like horseback riding," she said. "And that means he can't be in The Saddle Club."

"Not even honorary?" Stevie suggested.

"No," Carole said. "He's nice and he can be our friend, but Lisa's right. He doesn't qualify. Being horse crazy is essential."

"He is pretty good at the helping-others part, though, isn't he?" Lisa asked. "That magic show was fabulous."

"Definitely," Stevie agreed. "Skye was helpful with all the planning of the party. He can pitch in on Saddle Club projects anytime he wants."

The girls were quiet for a minute, enjoying the gentle sound of the babbling water, the wind playing with the branches of the trees, and the horses munching lazily on stray strands of grass that grew by the brook.

Lisa felt totally content. It wasn't the exciting and wonderful feeling of Skye's magic show, or the surreal one she'd experienced while she was involved with the movie. It was just a feeling of happiness and peace. It was a very nice, very normal feeling. She was happy to be with her friends and their horses.

"Okay," Stevie said abruptly, "so now the movie's over, the party's finished, and we're even done with the cleaning up. What are we going to do for excitement?"

Carole and Lisa laughed. It was just like Stevie to be thinking about the next project at a quiet moment. Stevie didn't enjoy quiet moments as much as Lisa and Carole did.

"We could just sit here and talk about horses," Lisa suggested.

"Or we could practice some of the riding skills we didn't get to practice this week because the riding classes were canceled," Carole suggested.

"I've got an idea!" Stevie announced. "Why don't we work on our next project?"

"And what's that going to be?" Carole asked, mildly curious.

"Why your father's fiftieth birthday party, of course!" Stevie said.

Pepper had an answer for that. Almost as if he understood what was going on, he snorted loudly. It sounded just like a raspberry.

Carole and Lisa laughed. Stevie joined in.

Everything was very normal. Everything was very good.

ABOUT THE AUTHOR

BONNIE BRYANT is the author of many books for young readers, including novelizations of movie hits such as *Teenage Mutant Ninja Turtles®* and *Honey, I Blew Up the Kid*, written under her married name, B. B. Hiller.

Ms. Bryant began writing The Saddle Club in 1986. Although she had done some riding before that, she intensified her studies then and found herself learning right along with her characters Stevie, Carole, and Lisa. She claims that they are all much better riders than she is.

Ms. Bryant was born and raised in New York City. She still lives there, in Greenwich Village, with her two sons.

SNOW RIDE
THE SADDLE CLUB #20

When Stevie is invited to Vermont to visit her friend
Dinah for the annual sugaring-off event, she's not sure
that she wants to leave the rest of The Saddle Club behind.
But then she finds out that Dinah's riding class is having
a contest to see which team can gather the most sap, and
Stevie can't resist the challenge. She's also thrilled to learn
that Dinah has arranged for the two of them to ride the
Rocky Road trail, a difficult but beautiful trail that's off-
limits to certain riders. Dinah isn't exactly experienced
enough for the trail, but she convinces Stevie to help her,
and they both promise not to tell a soul. When an accident happens on the Rocky Road trail, Stevie knows that
they have made a mistake. But what should she do: keep
the secret or tell the truth?

Help your friend get FREE books and FREE gifts - by joining The Saddle Club!

As an official Saddle Club member, you'll get:

- A beautiful keepsake diary
- An official Saddle Club poster
- A stunning charm bracelet and Saddle Club charms
- Plus much, much more!